Before My Breath is Scattered

Discovering Resilience & Renewal

KIMISOO KIM

This writing is a fictional or reconstructed account based on actual events or imagined situations.

The characters, institutions, locations, incidents, and backgrounds mentioned in the text are unrelated to reality and have no connection to any real events or individuals.

Copyright © 2024 Gavotte Inc.

All rights reserved.

Including the right of reproduction in whole or in part in any form.

ISBN: 978-0-9912898-9-9

New York, New York

First Edition, December 25, 2024

To my darling daughter, whom I love with all my heart and breath.

CONTENTS

ACKNOWLEDGMENTS i

ME: 1
   Mommy Papillon 2

WITH MY DAUGHTER: 18
   If God Asks 19
   Same Routine 30
   New Routine 33
   Extra Routine 37
   Mommy's Shared Notes 42
      Note 1 - Mistake 42
      Note 2 - Promise 42
      Note 3 - Listen 43
      Note 4 - Breakfast 44
      Note 5 - Prepare 44
      Note 6 - Shoelaces 46
      Note 7 - Crayon 47
      Note 8 - Juice 48
      Note 9 - Book 49
      Note 10 - Words 50
      Note 11 - Respect 51
      Note 12 - Precious 52
      Note 13 - Play 53
      Note 14 - Sharing 55
      Note 15 - Fight 55
      Note 16 - Filter 56
      Note 17 - Praise 59
   Ugly Duckling Is Not Your Real Name 63

   Mothers Groups 67
      The Anonymous Letter: 67
      Morning Coffee with the Moms: 73
      Always being with a close mother: 80
      Why do you walk everywhere? 84

   I Don't Know How To Use a Dyson 88

THEIR LIVES: 99

- Different Thoughts 1 100
- Different Thoughts 2 110
- Different Thoughts 3 116
- Different Thoughts 4 123

MY LIFE: 130

- A Freelancer is Not Free 131
- Discovering The Outlaws 138
- Abduction 146
- Returning 152
- Why Do I Still Wear a Mask? 156
- Breakfast with the Mayor 164
- First Accident 171
- Pee Pads 180
- Lingering at a Shopping Mall 186
- The Last Makeup 192
- Since 198
  - Things I Can Do Laying Down ················198
  - It Hurts More Because It's in Korean ··········206
  - Signing to Stay Alive ························210
- Afterwards 215
  - Do everything you want to do. ················215
  - Dreams exist because they can be dreamt. ········220
  - A Human Water Drop ···························224
  - The only thing I can do is write. ··············228
- The Days Spent Lying Down During the Pandemic 233
- Courage on the Ground 239

NOW: 246

- I Am Trying Not to Rely on Tranquilizers 247
  - The Threat in Manhattan ······················247
  - The Nightmare on the Highway ·················249
  - The Miracle in Subzero Weather ···············250
  - The German Car Mishap ························252
  - The Collision on the Road ····················253

At the Hospital ER ····························256
  Being Alive ···································258
  Amidst the Endless Pain ·······················260

Peace in the Noise of Starbucks 262

Today Marks 98 Days 272

Don't Buy Thoughts of Worry Like I Do in Life 278

Life Unfolds Through Encounters 287

SCRIBBLED EMOTIONS DAY BY DAY: ············296

  Day 1 - Life 297
  Day 2 - Appreciating 298
  Day 3 - Wounds 299
  Day 4 - Moment 300
  Day 5 - Wrap 301
  Day 6 - Existence 302
  Day 7 - Blame 303
  Day 8 - Relationship 305
  Day 9 - Character 306
  Day 10 - Like That 307
  Day 11 - Difference Between Pain and Suffering ... 308
  Day 12 - Rest 310
  Day 13 - Play 311
  Day 14 - Now 312
  Day 15 - Much 315
  Day 16 - Again 316
  Day 17 - One Thing 317
  Day 18 - Boundary Between Tears & Sorrow 318
  Day 19 - Head 320
  Day 20 - Gone 321
  Day 21 - Strong 322
  Day 22 - Next 323
  Day 23 - Last 324
  Day 24 - I Write 326

Day 25 - First Snow 328
Day 26 - Alone! 329
Day 27 - Your Choice 330
Day 28 - Holding 332
Day 29 - Reaction 334
Day 30 - Even Tonight 336
Day 31 - Expectation 339
Day 32 - Same 340
Day 33 - Pain 341
Day 34 - Irony 342
Day 35 - Human 345
Day 36 - Thought's End? 347
Day 37 - The Boundary Between Emotion and Attitude . 348
Day 38 - Let Go 351
Day 39 - Laugh 352
Day 40 - Habit 354
Day 41 - Position 355
Day 42 - Interpretation 356
Day 43 - See 359
Day 44 - Difference? 360
Day 45 - Expression 361
Day 46 - Traces 363
Day 47 - Find Me 364
Day 48 - On Three Legs 365

ABOUT THE AUTHOR ···························· 370

ACKNOWLEDGMENTS

My ever-reliable "Android" daughter played an indispensable role in shaping every aspect of this book, providing unwavering insight and support throughout the journey. My man, the "Alien," was equally instrumental in bringing this project to life.

"If you're reading these imperfect words, you must be either patient or wise."

"To read my words

is to sit with imperfection.

Thank you

for being willing."

Life itself is a story.

For some, it flows along a very ordinary and tranquil plotline. For others, every scene is a continuous series of challenges and surprises. Perhaps life can be seen as a book where these two elements are intertwined. Experiences that are a bit too abundant to be called ordinary, yet a reality too vivid to be called a novel.

This book captures the stories of a writer, a designer, a mother... who has walked an uncommon path.

ME :

Before My Breath is Scattered

Mommy Papillon

I cannot list all the words that could describe my life...
but here, in no particular order, are the ones that come to mind:

Korean-American • Parsons • Apple Island • Boxer M.A. • Fashion • Manhattan • Bodyguard • Public Figure • Cargo Airline • Lady Sashimi • California • Surgery • Paralysis • Rear-end Collision • Anesthesia • Spinal Injection • Trauma • Tranquilizers • The New School • The Big Apple • White Cane • Actor J.D. • Celebrity • Funeral • Air Rifle • Cipriani NYC • New York Daily News •

Before My Breath is Scattered

Intelligence Agency • Abduction • Politician • The New York Times • Prime Minister • Carnegie Hall NYC • Japan • NYU • Professor • Time Out New York • Writing • Notes • Traumatic Injury • Disability • Crutches • My Daughter...

And then...

From a place called New Yorking in Manhattan, I walked out of the restroom only to have someone suddenly point a gun at me.

Another time, as we finished a meal and waited to hail a taxi, a black box-like car suddenly stopped in front of us.

Before My Breath is Scattered

Inside the car, including the driver, were four men.

Once, biker gangs began to surround the car as we were driving.

On one winter day, while pregnant, I was walking slowly along a snowy path when suddenly all the strength drained from my body, and I collapsed to the ground.
I descended gently, like a fallen leaf, until I landed on the earth.

Looking back,
was it because my life is extraordinary?
Was I born under a rare and special fate?
Or did it happen because of the unique people I met?

Before My Breath is Scattered

Maybe the particular places I've been?

In my early 30s, I found myself in the company of a prince in exile from a small kingdom, a man who was his close friend, and an upper classmate from Parsons. We four were all gathered in the same dining space, at the same time, despite being from entirely different backgrounds, meeting for the first time.

The man and I, unexpectedly connected by our shared Korean heritage, met as man and woman and, after a single turn of the four seasons, were married.

'Mil-wol' (밀월/蜜月) is the Korean name for "honeymoon" and a baby born after a

honeymoon trip. Rather than "honeymoon baby," I prefer the melodic Korean pronunciation of 'mil-wol-agi'.
At Cornell University hospital on Apple Island, it was morning of April 20XX. I lay in a private labor room surrounded by doctors and nurses, while the man held my hand tightly. I could hear the steady hum of various machines, their sounds blending into the rhythm of a heartbeat. Labor began, and as my body prepared to welcome the baby, I followed the doctor's instructions and pushed.

The pain was intense, so much so that I was given a long, thin epidural needle in my spine. I did not scream. I was afraid the loud noise might frighten my baby...

Sweat dripping, I simply focused on pushing, following instructions.
Finally, it ended with a cry.
The cry sounded like an echo, as though my baby was calling out to me.
I could hear it clearly,
a moment of tearful joy and overwhelming emotion.

I caught a glimpse of the soft white blanket swaddling the baby.
"It is called Kuddle Up," they said.
– "It means to embrace."
This blanket, with its white fabric adorned by pink and blue candy stripes, has been a tradition since 1950, used in maternity wards everywhere.

Before My Breath is Scattered

It is something of a keepsake for mothers.

Wrapped in that blanket, wearing a thin
knit hat of the same colors,
the nurse handed my baby to me.
Taking a moment to catch my breath,
I instinctively prepared to nurse.
The baby's eyes remained closed,
but a few seconds later, she opened her
mouth and began nursing,
guided by pure instinct.
Slowly, her eyes began to open.
It was the first time we locked eyes.
While nursing, she gazed up at me,
her small, luminous eyes reflecting me
back.
It was an indescribably moving moment.

Before My Breath is Scattered

The birth of my daughter was a transformative milestone, marking the divide between the life I lived before becoming a mother and the life that began thereafter.

As a human, as a woman,
I left behind my own name...
Kimisu is of fictional origin and means "Child of the Heavens."
- "Kimisoo," a name inspired by literature, carries the meaning of an angel.

Is it mere coincidence that I was born on October 4th, a day associated with celestial meanings? "10-04" can be read as 'chun-sa' (천사/天使) in Korean, which translates to "angel." This name will remain with me as an eternal symbol.

But now, I am a mother.

From this day forward, my life begins anew, as the mother of my daughter, her name forever linked with mine.

On the day of my daughter's birth, my man suggested we hire private security for protection.

We also agreed on codenames: I was *Angel*, he was *Alien*, and our daughter was *Android*.

During a few other times when safety was a concern, we traveled with plainclothes security provided by a private firm. They ensured our protection by blending into the environment and maintaining a low profile.

After the first full cycle of four seasons had passed, after celebrating my daughter's first birthday, and after she had grown safely to her second, just a few months later, we were uprooted. Because of business, we had to leave Apple Island, a place I had never imagined leaving, for Orange Town, California, a place I had never imagined going. The very place I thought we would live forever, we now had to leave. The moment I heard the news, a single thought overwhelmed me: "Why is this happening to me?"

Before My Breath is Scattered

I had lived my entire life in cities, from the day I was born. I loved the forest of skyscrapers soaring into the sky, the diversity of people from every walk of life, their endless movement in the streets. I loved the energy of it all—the buses, the subways, the car service always ready wherever I needed them.

It was an active, dynamic life, vibrant and alive in every way. Living here, I could experience the profound rhythm of all four seasons, the essence of nature's vast cycle.

I could feel the pulse of the world itself in this city where everything existed. I was so deeply happy to live this city life, to live here, to call this my home.

I cried and cried, tears flowing endlessly, like water from an untended faucet. For the first time, I truly understood the phrase, "I feel like I'm losing my mind." But for my daughter, for the family that binds us together, I had no choice. This was a decision I could not refuse.

The weather in California is said to be mostly warm, even in winter—though it can be cold, it only feels like the early days of fall with occasional rain. In Orange Town, where we are to live, I've heard there are basic stores nearby. But regardless of the surrounding environment, the biggest problem lies with me: I can't drive. I'm terrified of driving. And life in California without driving is said to be unimaginable. A distance that would take no more than two or three minutes by car could take 10, 20, or even 30 minutes on foot. I can already picture myself, one hand holding my daughter's, the other gripping the stroller handle as we walk along. Like a hamster running in circles on a wheel in its cage, I imagine myself confined to the small bounds of Orange Town, endlessly walking. Like a duckling following its mother, my daughter and I would trudge along. And the more I think about it, the more my head fills with

Before My Breath is Scattered

this image: walking distances that could rival the steps it takes to reach the summit of the Himalayas—walking not because I want to, but because I must, to live, to survive.

In that place, with my nearly three-year-old daughter, the one who gives me breath, we will begin a new life—one that starts with walking. I can't count it, I can't predict it, and I can't escape it. So I marked each passing day on the calendar, clinging to the fervent hope that one day we'll leave this place and return to Apple Island. Until that day arrives, I only see myself trapped in my small pond—a place where I need no bodyguards, where no one knows me, and

Before My Breath is Scattered

where I am anonymous. Here, in this unfamiliar and disquieting place, my life as 'Mommy Papillon' begins anew.

WITH MY DAUGHTER:

If God Asks

If by chance

God were to ask,

"Does hell exist?"

I would answer like this:

"It is a place one can go when life ends..."

If God were to ask,

"Does heaven exist?"

I would answer like this:

"It is a place one can go when life ends..."

Why should we accept the existence of a place we go to when life is over?

Before My Breath is Scattered

I would answer that this is a place that exists in reality,
a place we can go to while alive,
a place that could be hell,
a place that could be heaven,
a place like that.

With surroundings and seasons that are completely different by 180 degrees...
With lifestyles and cultures that are completely different by 180 degrees...
A place where everything in the world is encountered rapidly and first...
Where the sounds of police cars and fire trucks are signatures, heard every day without fail...
Where white steam rises from street manholes...

Before My Breath is Scattered

This is the bustling, absolutely sleepless life of Apple Island...

From my life...
From my existence...
Leaving behind all the time I have lived, my daughter, born nearly three years ago, who allows me to continue to breathe, arriving with my man on the land of California, a new beginning of life to be embraced...

We arrived at the local airport in California. I just sighed. It was all just agony.
My whole body is suffocated. First, we retrieved our luggage and headed to the designated gate, to book an Uber to the

hotel. I just felt everything was uncomfortable and unpleasant.
However, seeing my daughter, all bright and excited by the new environment and the airplane ride, I couldn't help it. I could feel my pain and distress ease.

After a quick wash, we unpacked our luggage a bit and ordered room service. It seemed my man ordered wine for me. When the room service arrived, our daughter fiddled with a tiny ketchup bottle. Its cute size seemed adorable even to her eyes. After the meal, our family, tired from the long flight and struggling to adjust to the time difference, drifted off to dreamland right away.

Before My Breath is Scattered

The next morning, we moved into the townhouse my man had arranged. A few hours later, the moving truck arrived as scheduled. The movers brought in our boxes and did some basic organizing. On our second day here, we spent our first night in the house that would be our home. Everything felt strange to me. I'm just saddened by it all. It still feels difficult to adjust.

Our daughter wandered around, trotted here and there and even running with her little steps. She is delighted every time she opens a box with her belongings. We had a simple dinner with food my man picked up. As time passed and the night grew darker, my sadness deepened. My man was too busy unpacking to notice.

Before My Breath is Scattered

The night is incredibly dark. Because of that, the stars in the night sky seem to shine even brighter. However, in my heart, I only feel cold like tiny frozen icicles.

It feels like sad emotions will come and find me.

And I silently cry out in my heart. I hate this place so much... To me, who is alive, this place feels like hell...

My daughter, now tired and whining, starts to make a fuss. I lie down with her on the bed, hoping to settle her to sleep. After she falls asleep, fearful my sadness might be conveyed... scared she might hear me crying... I shift to my side, leaving space between us, and lie at the edge of the bed. It was a dark, quiet, and terrible night.

It was the first time in my life that I used the word "desolation." All the thoughts and emotions I could feel seemed to rush towards me as if they had been waiting. Tears flowed endlessly as if they had been held back. My nose ran endlessly as well. After wiping my nose and tears, my face felt sore from the dried marks.

My eyes were so swollen that when I opened them, it felt like I was looking through tiny slits, like the eyes of an ant. I could hear sounds and my man seemed to be organizing boxes. After what felt like an endless amount of time, when my tears finally ran dry, I naturally came to the realization that I needed to release the agony, sadness, anger, and despair that filled my thoughts and emotions.

As I looked at my sleeping daughter, I realized I had to endure this reality moving forward. Suddenly, I recalled something my man had said, "It may feel unfamiliar and take time, but it will be okay..."

Ultimately, I realized that the only person I could rely on emotionally and mentally in this place was myself, even though I didn't want to admit it. Apart from my family, I had no one. I didn't know anyone here. It was entirely unfamiliar since it was my first time here. I had to constantly remind myself and reaffirm my resolve.

Than before:
I must become a more stronger person.
I need to attain more greater mental composure and maturity.
I should cultivate more emotional flexibility within my heart.
I need to hold onto more respect and confidence in myself.

Going forward:
I might become vulnerable in this new environment.

Before My Breath is Scattered

I might be affected suddenly and feel bewildered by unexpected and confusing influences.
I might feel loneliness trapped in unseen spaces.
For everything, adapting to it with positive responses will be necessary.

From now on:
I must overcome and handle things with grace.
I already know that I can do it.
I must keep my mind and spirit healthy and true to myself.
These are the affirmations and sources of courage that only I can give.

Before My Breath is Scattered

From that first night, a glimmer of hope started to emerge in the darkness, knowing that I could rely on myself, my courage, and my determination as "Mommy Papillon." I began to believe that one day I would leave this place, and from that muddy, darker-than-night, desolate evening, hope started to blossom within me.

Same Routine

At around 8:00-8:30 in the morning, I see my man off.

This marks the start of the day for me and my daughter.

After a simple breakfast, I hold my daughter's hand in one and a stroller in the other as we step outside.

In our current reality, there are very few activities available to us.

However, I want to give my daughter a sense of choice.

So, I ask her,

"Should we go to the playground? Or should we go look at books?"

When my daughter responds, "Books," we walk to the Barnes & Noble bookstore.

Before My Breath is Scattered

After a 15-minute walk, we arrive, and my daughter starts running with excitement.

Inside, she begins pulling books off the shelves.

Once she finishes with the ones she's chosen, she picks more.

Sometimes, she flips through the pages on her own, simply looking at the pictures.

Other times, she asks me to read to her.

We sit together in the children's section, reading.

When it's near lunchtime, we go to the café inside Barnes & Noble.

For her, I get a sandwich and juice; for myself, a cup of coffee.

After she's had her fill and left part of the sandwich, I finish it with a single bite.

Then we return to the children's section. She resumes pulling books off the shelves, flipping through them.
Soon, she tells me she's sleepy—it's time for her nap.
As I prepare to put her in the stroller, she raises her arms, asking to be carried.
So, I hold her in one arm while pushing the stroller with the other as we head home.
By then, it's already 3:00 PM.

This routine repeated every single day during the first year of my life with my three-year-old daughter.

Then my daughter turned four.

New Routine

In the U.S., education generally starts at age four with preschool, age five with kindergarten, and age six with first grade in elementary school.

My daughter, who had spent every moment of her life with me since birth, was now at this threshold.

As her mother, I raised her with a focus on teaching and nurturing her character. But understanding the importance of group interaction and communal life,

I decided to enroll her in preschool.

In Orange Town, a Montessori preschool was located about a 30-minute walk away. I registered her there.

Before My Breath is Scattered

Other mothers drove their children, dropping them off in the mornings.

Since I didn't drive, I had to wake my daughter earlier than usual, get her ready, and walk the 30 minutes to the school.

Even when woken early, she would get up without any fuss, which made me proud.

Yet, a part of my heart ached.

After dropping her off, I would walk the 30 minutes back home to tend to my own tasks.

When the alarm rang, signaling pickup time, I walked the same route again to pick her up.

Holding her hand, we would walk the 30 minutes back home.

Before My Breath is Scattered

Now, walking hand in hand with my daughter for 30 minutes to Montessori in the morning has become more leisurely.
Waking up early in the morning, getting ready for school, and walking while looking at various flowers, trees, and the blue sky.
We even see a hummingbird like the one in Disney's Pocahontas.
It looks exactly the same. So tiny. Its wings flapping so fast. They are almost invisible.
My daughter loves it and finds it fascinating.
As we walked, we even discovered a snail. It was slow, so slow.
Though these are trivial discoveries, they bring immense happiness to me and my

daughter. Even though we see the same things every day, to us, they appear fresh and new each time.

Extra Routine

One day, my daughter said she wanted to learn ballet.

I signed her up.

In the morning, when I take her to school, I pack her ballet outfit and shoes as well.

I walk back home and take care of my tasks, and when the pick-up time comes, the alarm goes off.

Once again, I walk 30 minutes to arrive at Montessori.

I help my daughter change her clothes and shoes, then send her off to the new ballet studio next to Montessori.

I have to wait for 45 minutes.

There's a small glass window on the door of the studio.
Mothers gather there, peeking in to watch their children.
I wanted to see as well, but I only glanced for a few seconds before moving to another space.

I saw a bench and decided to sit down.
Looking at the time, I realized there were still 40 minutes left.
I took out a book that belonged to my daughter from my bag.
Since there was still time left, I went to the reading area inside Montessori.
I simply pulled out a book that caught my eye and began reading.

Before My Breath is Scattered

From across the room, I could hear other mothers chatting together.

As I was reading, my phone rang.
It was my daughter.
"Mommy~ aren't you coming to pick me up?"
I had completely forgotten.
I rushed to the ballet studio right away.

From that day on, reading books while waiting became part of my routine.
It felt different from when I read books with my daughter at Barnes & Noble.

Then I found out: Among the other mothers at Montessori, they referred to me with a few nicknames:

"The mom who can't drive," "the walking mom," "the mom who plays alone," and "the book mom."

Now that my daughter is four years old and attends Montessori from Monday to Friday, if she wants to go read books, we visit Barnes & Noble on Saturdays.
Before that, we used to go nearly 4-5 times a week.
My daughter and I would arrive at the bookstore at 11:00 a.m. and read books together. We'd have lunch at the Starbucks café inside and then read more. Sometimes, my daughter would open and close the books she had picked out, lost in thought.
I would simply watch in silence.

Before My Breath is Scattered

Eventually, she would hand me a book, saying she wanted to bring it home. I'd use the Barnes & Noble membership card for a discount, pay for the book, and hand it to her. If she wanted to go home or take a nap, we would usually walk back home around 2:00 or 3:00 p.m.

My daughter and I have spent countless hours and days at Barnes & Noble, living through time together with books. We also became close with Helen, one of the bookstore staff, and shared those years with her as well.

Even after years of doing the same routine, for my daughter and me, it never felt boring.

Each day felt fresh and new, even though it was the same routine.

Mommy's Shared Notes

Note 1 - Mistake

Mom also makes mistakes with her child.
I can't remember all of my child's belongings.
I mistook the things I couldn't remember for items my child had forgotten outside and scolded my child.
Can you offer an apology along with a gentle explanation to your child?

Note 2 - Promise

Mom couldn't keep the promise to play with the child.
Keeping promises is one of the fundamental elements that give trust and faith as a human being.

Can you offer a beautiful apology to your child, not with excuses or lightly brushing it off, but by explaining the reason why you couldn't keep the promise?

Note 3 - Listen

Mom says the child isn't listening.
But as an adult, Mom believes she is always right and never wrong.
And then, Mom makes a conclusion.
Because of this, she can't hear the voice of the child's heart.
What does the child want?
What does the child need?
Why is the child crying?
Can you listen to the child's heart, adjusting to the child's level of understanding?

Note 4 - Breakfast

The child eats breakfast before going to kindergarten.

They eat slowly.

It's not that they're doing something else.

Mom is in a hurry.

She wants to feed them more.

She grabs the spoon and feeds the child.

Usually, you know your child eats slowly.

What if you wake the child a bit earlier and let them eat at their own pace?

Then, both Mom's and the child's hearts will have a more relaxed morning routine.

Note 5 - Prepare

In the morning, Mom chooses the child's clothes.

Before My Breath is Scattered

The child wants to wear the clothes they picked.

Mom wants the child to wear the clothes Mom chose.

Looking at the clock, Mom starts to feel anxious.

She hurriedly puts on the clothes Mom picked.

The child begins to cry and feels upset.

Mom is also upset by the child's tears but is too flustered to think clearly.

Mom picks up the child, puts on the kindergarten bag, and runs.

Usually, you know that every morning, you and the child have a struggle over choosing clothes.

After dinner, check the weather for the next day.

What if you choose clothes together with your child and decide in advance?
Then, both hearts can start the day with happy and relaxed steps to kindergarten.

Note 6 - Shoelaces

Mom must wait for the child to try something.

She must wait.

Because it is through this that the child gains confidence and a sense of accomplishment.

Some moms, feeling impatient, can't wait for the child to try and instead do it for them right away.

The child tries to tie their shoelaces with small hands.

Mom says, "I'll tie it nicely for you," and ties the laces herself.

Can you wait until the child ties their own shoelaces?

Note 7 - Crayon

The child is coloring.

It's a simple picture, but the child is happily coloring with enthusiasm.

The pace is slow.

Choosing the crayon colors is also slow.

Mom feels frustrated.

Mom sits next to the child, chooses the colors, and colors together, turning to the next page.

Can you wait until the child finishes coloring?

Note 8 - Juice

The child asks for juice, juice!

Mom hands the child a juice pack.

The child sits down, and tears open the straw.

Slowly, they peel off the plastic.

After removing it, the child blows on the straw.

It is fun.

Then, the child attempts to insert the straw.

The juice box topples over.

But the child continues to try.

Mom thinks to herself, "This will take all day."

Mom approaches the child.

Saying "Like this~" she gently inserts the straw.

Can you wait until the child inserts the straw on their own?

Note 9 - Book

The child sits down, looking at a number book, reading slowly.

Mom feels very proud.

Mom brings over a newly purchased number book.

She sits beside the child and begins teaching.

The child wants to do something else.

The child refuses.

Mom thinks to herself,

"Is it too hard?

Is it difficult?

Does the book not interest them?

Did I buy the wrong one?"

Thoughts swirl in her brain.

She needs to think from the child's perspective.

The child has their own opinions.

Can you wait for the child's opinion?

Note 10 - Words

The child may have something they want, but they might only say it to themselves.

They may want to speak, but their words could be unsteady.

They might be angry, but only make noise.

They could be excited and only make noise.

They might know they've done something wrong and cry, afraid of being scolded.

They might say a few words and then remain silent.

The child is still learning to express their feelings.

Can you wait and listen until the child finishes speaking?

Note 11 - Respect

> "When talking to your little one, kneel or squat down to their eye level."

There are two meanings here.

When talking to your child,

you speak at their eye level,

so that they feel a sense of security and understand that they are receiving attention.

Next, when talking to your child,

you need to consider their position and age and engage in conversation from their perspective.

Even though they are young, a child is an individual and should be respected as such.

Note 12 - Precious

My precious child.

So, the child's belongings should be cherished as well.

Mom is cleaning.

She knows it's the child's belongings.

In Mom's reasoning, it seems like something to throw away.

The child probably won't notice, right?

There's so much of it!

It doesn't seem necessary.

If the child needs something, we can just buy it again!

But the child also has an opinion.

It belongs to the child.

If you respect your child more than cleanliness or your own stubbornness, how about spending time together organizing and cleaning up their things?

Note 13 - Play

There may be mothers who think or say things like this:

"I need to play with my child!"

"I play with my child because I love them!"

"All the other moms do it too!"

These expressions are not positive.

They are conditional expressions.

Children are pure.

They accept everything from their mothers.

A child will feel happiness in activities and expressions that involve their mother, responding alongside her.

A child will be overjoyed just holding their mother's hand and walking together.

A child finds fun even in the silly sounds their mother makes.

A child feels protected and secure simply by being hugged by their mother.

Starting out as a parent can be clumsy, and things may not go as planned.

With the desire to do well as a mother, trying to fit everything into a rigid framework that you've created can leave you feeling exhausted and strained.

What if, instead, you and your child could learn and grow together?

Note 14 – Sharing

At the playground, many children are waiting their turn to ride the swings. One mom says, "Just a little bit more, just a little bit more... it'll be fine!" and continues pushing their child on the swing.
A thoughtful mom would not do this from the beginning.

Note 15 - Fight

At the playground,
Your child walks over to you, crying after being hit by another child. You feel deeply upset.

Your heart hurts, and you might feel angry.

As a mom, what is the first thing you would say to your child?

"Did you hit them too?"

"Why did you just take it?"

"Who did this?"

A wise mom, however, would not say any of these things at first.

Note 16 - Filter

Meeting with moms,

Endless chatting where time flies, and the parting words,

"I'll text you later!"

Relaxing with coffee and brunch, feeling content, and the parting words,

Before My Breath is Scattered

"Shall we go to that trendy Instagram-famous place next time?"

In the morning, moms drop their children off at kindergarten or school, and this is their main daily routine.

The greatest joy in gatherings of moms is chatting, and the topics are limitless, with no boundaries in sight.

There are no limits to how much one should listen to or accept the things said by other moms.

In the stories shared among moms, there may be right things, wrong things, or exaggerated things.

Because of this, someone may end up feeling upset or going through difficult situations.

When something like this happens to you, you might think, "I trusted too much."
You might blame the other mom or the person you were with.
However, it is no one's fault.
It is something you yourself accepted.
It is the result of decisions you made based on your own thoughts.
The simple stories shared among moms, the everyday conversations, are part of daily life, but they also require attention.
Think of it like a water purifier, filtering or accepting what comes through.
The recognition and value you place on these conversations with other moms is something only you can decide.

Therefore, the recognition, the meaning you assign, and the consequences that come from them will be yours to bear.

Note 17 - Praise

Children and adults feel good when they receive praise. Receiving praise is a happy message from someone who acknowledges you, such as a parent.

From mom and dad, a child who grows up hearing praise at home will naturally develop a positive outlook and confidence in being acknowledged.

Even when giving small compliments to a child, it is essential to give the right kind of praise.
Praise should not be given carelessly or wrapped up in vague good meanings.
It should not be done lightly.
It could even have the opposite effect on the child.

When giving praise, it is more important to emphasize the process, effort, and practice the child is putting in, rather than just praising the result.

The outcome can be good, bad, or disappointing, as there are many possible answers.

Rather than the result, a child who is praised for the process of preparation and practice will learn the power of self-effort and become aware of their ability to challenge themselves.

This is what will create the strength and build confidence in their ability to try again and challenge oneself.

When giving praise, as a parent, doing so halfheartedly is worse than not doing it at all.

Because a child can feel their parents' true emotions.

Even if the child is young, the parents' facial expressions and voice are conveyed to the child's persona.

Because they absorb it.

The reason for the praise and the explanation should be conveyed with a sincere heart.

Ugly Duckling Is Not Your Real Name

Since you were born, your appearance and color were different from other ducks, so you were called Ugly Duckling.
But your heart held good innocence and beauty.
Ducks only saw the outside.
Baby Ugly Duckling, you were bullied and hurt by other ducks for looking different.

Although the mother duck loved and cared for you very much, you begin your journey to self-discovery on your own. With confidence, you set out.

Ugly Duckling came across a grandmother's house, and you spent time and suffered pain under the chickens and cats that lived there.

You grew and grew from experience after experience. Then one day, you saw your true form reflected in the water and realized how beautiful you were and how beautifully you had grown.

Although it's an old children's fairy tale, I look back, now as an adult, and see the story holds many meanings, one of which is the truth that everyone starts their life differently.

Before My Breath is Scattered

I live through life and, without realizing it, I am one of the ducks: Evaluating someone because they are different. Different. Wrong. Comparable. Unclean and Uncomfortable. These things live in my heart.

Or I am the Ugly Duckling: Discriminated against and treated unfairly because I am different. Different in appearance. Different in values. Judged.

Both coexisting.
All of these differences we cannot handle or overcome alone.

As human beings, we need to respect the diversity of each individual with a clear awareness and a healthy attitude.

Ducks who only look at the outside cannot recognize the inside of a true swan and the beauty that slowly materialize. It is impossible for them.

We live together as human beings, passing our legacy to the next generation.
In our society, we must accept and respect each other's appearance.

I hope that you will be able to see the invisible beauty within people with the eyes of your heart.

Mothers Groups

The Anonymous Letter:

One day, I received a phone call from Berry's mom. Berry's mom was someone I became acquainted with through the community of mothers. On the day I had registered my daughter at Montessori, she said to me, "Don't you frequent Barnes & Noble?" She recognized me and my daughter, remembering us from the times she had seen us walking together. As our only daughters ended up in the same class, it was natural for us to grow closer.

Berry's mom asked, "Did you receive a letter from an anonymous mother?"

I told her I hadn't. She suggested we meet at the children's ballet studio.

The contents of the anonymous letter described the heartache and distress of a mother living in Orange Town. It spoke of the ostracism she experienced from other mothers, the hardships she endured, and even included details about the personal family issues of certain mothers who had tormented her. The most shocking part of the letter was the story of the man of one of the so-called "privileged" mothers in the neighborhood.
This man was living a double life, maintaining two separate households. In each household, there were children of similar ages, and these children all

attended the same school. One day, there was an assignment for students to bring in family photos. As the children shared and compared their pictures, they discovered that they had shared the same father.

This incident had taken place several years prior. Yet, despite this scandal, the privileged mother had continued to associate with her clique, ostracizing and tormenting the mother who had written the anonymous letter. The letter concluded with the tormented mother pouring out her anguish, sending the letter to several mothers in Orange Town to express the bitterness and sorrow she carried in her heart.

Before My Breath is Scattered

For a time, the atmosphere in the town was tense. People tried to figure out who had written the letter, scrutinizing and suspecting one another. It was a deeply sorrowful situation.

One day, I saw the group of mothers described in the anonymous letter. They were still moving around together as if nothing had happened. I remembered something another mother had once said to me: that this clique referred to me as the "mom who can't drive," the "walking mom," the "mom who plays alone."
Later, a rumor began to circulate. Some mothers moved to different towns, and it was speculated that one of them was likely the author of the letter.

Regardless, as parents, as mothers, it is our duty to teach our children that bullying of any kind—whether among children or adults—is wrong and unacceptable. That such behavior could occur among mothers was not only heartbreaking but also an indication of immaturity.

Even now, I occasionally run into this group of mothers. On the mornings I walked my daughter to Montessori and headed back home, I sometimes see them riding together in a car. I can feel their eyes on me as they roll down the windows to stare. At the only supermarket in Orange Town, I also encounter them. I lift my head high, push my cart, and walk past them.

But I can hear them. Of course, I can. They make sure their words reach me. Yet, I choose not to react. After all, this is just who they are. It's their usual behavior.

One thing I've noticed about this group is that they never move around alone. Not a single one of them. Even if it's just two of them, they always stick together. That's their daily routine—always in a pack.

Morning Coffee with the Moms:

One morning, as I was leaving Montessori after dropping off my daughter, I ran into Berry's mom. She told me she was heading to have morning coffee with some of the other Montessori moms and invited me along, gently pulling me by the hand. I asked her where they were going. Thankfully, it was a bakery café nearby, within walking distance, so I agreed to join.

Inside the bakery café, groups of mothers were scattered across various tables. They all seemed incredibly busy, deeply engrossed in conversation. Laughter echoed here and there, and I saw them greeting one another warmly. Berry's mom led me to a table where a group of mothers she knew had already gathered. I didn't know their names, but I could tell which children they belonged to.

Soon, the chatter began—not so much casual conversation as a flood of words. Most conversations started with talk about the children. Mothers of accomplished children proudly boasted of their kids' achievements. Mothers of children struggling with something shared their frustrations. Some mothers simply sat quietly, listening. Others offered words of comfort and encouragement.
The topics naturally shifted. From education, teachers, and Montessori staff to personal family stories, mans, daily

meal plans, in-laws, sales at the mall, newly opened restaurants, stock investments, golf courses and coaches, cosmetics and their effects, TV dramas, celebrities... The range of subjects was endless, flowing without pause.

As the mothers exchanged stories, one mother began talking about Daisy's mom, who wasn't present. In that moment, all the other mothers focused entirely on her. Some mothers chimed in, agreeing. Others added more details to the story. A few admitted they already knew but had kept quiet. And still, there were mothers who urged her to stop talking.

At that moment, I found myself wondering why I was even sitting there. I had come along because I felt comfortable with Berry's mom and had built a personal connection with her, but these new faces, her friends, were unfamiliar to me, and I found it difficult to adapt. I just sat there, sipping my coffee, and listening.

Deep down, I knew I could easily join in and talk about another mother. But when I thought about basic manners and mutual respect, it didn't feel like the kind of conversation that should be had lightly. After all, one day, if you're not present, you could easily become the topic of conversation. A gathering where honest and respectful dialogue is exchanged, with a foundation of trust and mutual respect—that would be a mature meeting of mothers. But if the gathering is based on personal biases, invisible lines drawn to exclude or distinguish others, and friendships forged solely on shared attitudes, then it becomes an immature meeting.

After some time, the mothers began discussing where to move for lunch. They also started looking up a café for coffee afterward. I told Berry's mom that I'd have lunch at home because I needed to pick up my daughter. She suggested we have lunch together, then drive to the Montessori school. But I politely declined, saying I'd feel more at ease going home and then heading out later. I walked back home.

Berry's mom understood my feelings.

What defines a mother's gathering?
What is the meaning of these meetings?

I don't think the number of people gathering—three, five, or more—is important. If the meeting doesn't suit me or makes me uncomfortable, I don't believe I need to force myself to continue attending. Nor do I think I need to try hard to fit in or be included. If the purpose of joining such a group is to gather parenting or educational tips for my child, then the internet, reference books, and online parenting communities provide plenty of accurate information. I can also consult with teachers directly. Even among close mothers, not everything is shared openly.

A meeting where mutual respect exists, where there is comfort and understanding between mothers, is meaningful. A meeting with differing intentions or objectives might serve a different purpose. Ultimately, this is a decision each mother must make for herself. For me, attending mothers' gatherings has mostly been limited to public or necessary meetings, such as parent meetings at my daughter's Montessori school. After this experience, I stopped taking further steps into the circle of mothers.

This was both the first and the last time such an incident occurred in my life as a mother.

Always being with a close mother:
Today, I walked to pick up my daughter again. Upon arriving at the Montessori parking lot, I heard someone running toward me. It was Tulip's mom. Though she's a fellow mother, she's younger, slender, and undeniably beautiful—a mother whose appearance naturally draws compliments.

Before My Breath is Scattered

She hesitated for a moment before asking if I had some time to spare. Tulip's mom was clearly upset. She poured out her frustrations: Why hadn't her close mom-friend contacted her? Why had she arranged to meet other moms without her? Tulip's mom lamented, wondering if she'd done something wrong, and she continued to share her distress, one detail at a time. Then, she finally turned to me, awaiting my response.

I answered, "Tulip's mom, what kind of words are you hoping to hear from me right now? I'll text you after I get home, okay?"

Before My Breath is Scattered

After bringing my daughter home, I quickly bathed her, prepared her a snack, and then sat down to write a message. I wanted Tulip's mom to have the chance to read and process the words at her own pace, finding some calmness and reflection in the process. If my message helped her understand even a little and brought her some comfort, I would be relieved. If not, I'd still feel sorry for her situation. With these thoughts, I sent the message.

"Tulip's mom,
You can't always share everything with your close mom friends.

When my child makes a close friend, it's natural that I'll build a relationship with that child's mother. We might go shopping together, have lunch, do each other favors, or discuss matters about our children. That's how relationships grow closer.

But it's not always possible to share everything. There may be times when that close mom friend doesn't contact you, makes plans with other mothers, and doesn't inform you.

There's no need to feel upset or disappointed. There's no need to think negatively about it either. At times like these, just remind yourself that it's no big deal and carry on with your life as usual.

Mothers' relationships often revolve around their children. Depending on the situation, things can change at any time. But fundamentally, relationships built with wisdom, mutual respect, and careful communication will last peacefully."

Why do you walk everywhere?

During a small event at Montessori, mothers of children who attended the school gathered. Berry's mom slowly introduced me to the other mothers.

One mother cautiously asked me, "Why do you walk everywhere? Why don't you learn to drive?"

I wasn't offended; it was a natural question. After all, in California, driving is a necessity, and not being able to drive could easily seem unusual.

I answered, "I can't drive, but I do have a license. I got it a long time ago when I needed an ID. The written test wasn't an issue because I studied for it. For the driving test, I memorized everything—how to park, merge, turn, signal, stop at signs, and make road turns. I even memorized angles and timing down to the second. I passed the driving test on my first attempt. But I've never driven since because I'm too scared."

Then another mom asked, "What if your child gets sick? What if you need to take her to the hospital quickly?"

When I heard that, I wondered how to respond—emotionally or rationally?

I replied, "As a mom, I've prepared for emergencies. I have a stocked medical kit and studied how to handle basic situations. In an emergency, I'd contact my man or call 911. Besides, I always stay near my daughter—at home or close to her school."

Whether my answer was convincing or not, that was the truth. At that moment, Berry's mom jumped in, saying, "If anything happens, call me! I'm great at driving—fast and safe!" Everyone laughed, and the conversation ended there.

So far, my daughter has never experienced an emergency. For that, I am truly grateful.

Before My Breath is Scattered

I Don't Know How To Use a Dyson

I didn't know.

I couldn't feel it at all.

After picking up my daughter from Montessori, I returned home.

Suddenly, I started sweating, and blood began to flow.

It wasn't the start of a regular cycle.

In a rush, I searched for a dark towel.

I worried the sight of the blood might frighten my daughter.

I laid the towel on the sofa, covered myself, and lay down.

Thankfully, my daughter was in her room, changing the clothes of her doll.

Before My Breath is Scattered

It was still a while before my man could arrive, so our housekeeper came over immediately. She placed my daughter in the car seat and drove to the nearest OB-GYN clinic she could find. When we arrived, she waited with my daughter in the waiting room, while I was taken to the operating room by the nurses.

The doctor entered, and the nurses asked me questions in turns.
The doctor said it was a miscarriage.
A needle was inserted into my hand.
Multiple stickers were placed on my body, and then the sound began.
The sound, like a vacuum cleaner...
It began.

Before My Breath is Scattered

I could feel the sensation of suction,
as if the doctor was pulling something out.
I felt it in the place that had been my baby's home—my womb.
There was no anesthesia.
I felt every bit of pain, every cell in my body screaming.
The raw pain surged through me,
like someone was scraping and pulling at my very being.

I endured.
I could only endure.
I didn't make a sound.
I didn't scream.
I was more afraid that my daughter in the waiting room might hear my voice.

I only desperately hoped for this moment to end soon.

And then, there was a brief silence.
The doctor left a few words before leaving, "It's all done, and everything went cleanly. You did well."
The nurse said, "You endured very well."
After I had stabilized, they brought me out in a wheelchair.

The first thing I saw was my daughter's face.
I was just relieved that I could see her again.
That was all.

Before My Breath is Scattered

The housekeeper drove us back home and left after settling us in.
I lay in bed while my daughter fell asleep next to me.
Later, the housekeeper returned.
I thanked her profusely and expressed my gratitude.
She prepared a meal and then went back home.
I spoke briefly with my man over the phone,
and then tried to sleep again.
My daughter, nestled beside me, was sleeping so peacefully.

The next morning, my man took our daughter to Montessori.

Before My Breath is Scattered

Though I felt weak, I resolved to regain my energy,

thinking of how I wanted to pick her up later.

Text messages began to arrive.

One after another.

From Berry's mom, Tulip's mom—

a handful of moms I knew.

It turned out that another mom in our townhouse complex had seen me being helped into the car the day before.

She had passed the story along to others, and word had spread.

Only then did I understand the meaning behind their texts.

I made myself some warm green tea and sat on the sofa.

Why...

Before My Breath is Scattered

Why did she feel the need to share something she just happened to see?
Was it because her days were too dull?
Was she overly curious?
I thought about it briefly,
then sent a simple reply to Berry's mom, asking her to explain the situation to the other moms.
I set an alarm and lay down for a bit.

The alarm rang.
Slowly, I walked to pick up my daughter.
I saw the moms.
They came closer, offering their words of comfort:
    "It's okay!"
    "I heard miscarriages can feel like giving birth."

"Take care of yourself!"

"You'll be fine!"

"What can we do?"

"Let us know if you need anything!"

"Thank goodness you're okay!"

I picked up my daughter and answered them with a smile.

I had anticipated this, knowing the news wouldn't simply pass unnoticed.

Today felt like a long day packed into a short moment.

A few days passed.

In the morning, I dropped my daughter off at Montessori,

then slowly walked back home.

As usual, I saw a group of moms in a single car passing by together.

Before My Breath is Scattered

Berry's mom and a few others texted to check in again.
The alarm rang.
It was time to pick up my daughter.
When I arrived at Montessori,
everything was as it always had been.
Just like a fleeting midsummer night's dream,
the moment had passed.
Not one mom brought up the miscarriage anymore.
This must be the natural flow of life in the world of moms.

The greatest sorrow, the deepest pain of my life,
never returned to me.

Before My Breath is Scattered

From then on, it was just me and my daughter,

the one who keeps me breathing.

And since then, I've only ever used a broom and dustpan.

To this day, I don't know how to use a Dyson.

THEIR LIVES:

Different Thoughts 1

Life is...

Fate is...

While we are alive, the probability of meeting again by chance is...

The friend I first met in school on Apple Island.

The friend who picks out snacks for drinking.

The friend with pale skin and a strong spirit.

The friend with whom I exchanged occasional messages.

The friend who married before me.

The friend who, by chance, ended up at the same obstetrics clinic.

The friend with whom, even in silence, there was no awkwardness in the same space.

The friend who proudly boasted about receiving a foreign-brand sedan as a gift from her father-in-law after giving birth to her son, that friend.

The friend who always talked about the things she received because her husband's family was wealthy.

But that friend had pain. It was because of her husband's infidelity. Later, that friend told me, "If only I had known everything beforehand, I would have understood why I received so much. The woman lived in the apartment above, and my husband lived in the one below."

Before My Breath is Scattered

That friend could no longer understand it. Due to her wealthy in-laws, she gave up custody, agreed to a divorce with a substantial settlement, and consented to the divorce, with a new identity, left for the foreign country she had always wanted to live in, leaving only a final message. After that, I never heard from her again.

I arrived at the elementary school to pick up my daughter, walking just like any other day. I exchanged brief greetings with a few familiar moms and stood waiting for the kids to come out. At that moment, a man—no, a father—walked toward us, holding a pouch in his hand. He stood out because of his tall stature.

Among the moms, the one with the loudest voice and the fastest gossip, Carrie's Mom, began speaking. She said that he was a wealthy father who had remarried, bringing with him a son and a new wife. She mentioned that he owned several businesses and that the rumors about him had already spread widely among the local moms.

But the tall man with the pouch — he was that friend's ex-husband. I was simply shocked. It was absurd, but that seemed to be all. They say the world is small, but how could it be... That friend's son was attending the same elementary school as my daughter.

Before My Breath is Scattered

On the way home after picking up my daughter, I ran into my friend's ex-husband and his son. They lived in the villa next to ours. My daughter and his son seemed to know each other, exchanging greetings. I couldn't avoid exchanging a simple greeting as well.

The ex-husband of my friend said, "I saw you walking with your daughter. If it's alright with you, since we live in the villa next door, your son and mine could ride together to school in the morning."

I thought to myself, "Really...? No..." I just calmly declined and went inside the house with my daughter. He didn't recognize me, but I recognized him.

After that, I continued to hear rumors about my friend's ex-husband. I heard that his parents were taking care of his son together. His mother-in-law was apparently unusually dedicated to her grandson. It seems that she had even had a few arguments with some of the other mothers.

Before his remarriage, he had been seeing a single mom. But at the same time, he was also meeting the woman he eventually married. The single mom found out about it, so my friend's ex-husband unilaterally told her that they should break up in order for him to remarry. He also set her up with a small store, as a gesture of comfort, and these details were secretly shared by a real estate agent. The single mom, devastated by the situation, was rumored to have suffered a decline in her health as a result.

After hearing this, I realized that the single mom was the kind and gentle Sky's mom, whom I already knew. She lived in the same town villa, and her son went to the same school. Sky's mom had approached me first, and that's how we became acquainted. For a while, Sky's mom had trouble speaking clearly and had difficulty moving her hands. Before I knew about all this, I thought it was just complications from an illness, but now I realized the whole story.

Although many years have passed, everything about that old Apple Island friend had already disappeared. As a mother now, and as a friend, I think of her. I hope her son grows up happy and healthy...

Six years passed in California, and after returning to Apple Island, life in the city continued to move on. One day, I received a text from the mother of a child who had attended Montessori with mine in Orange Town. She said something had happened. She sent me a photo of an article through text, and that's how I found out.

It was an article related to that friend's ex-husband. The article was about him and a well-known female broadcaster. How could this happen... How far would this go... I was at a loss for words.

As a human living a life, there are basic principles that should be followed, including human instincts and reason— these things, when chosen and acted upon as personal preferences or tendencies, left traces in the private life of that friend's ex-husband...
It seems that people don't change.
That friend's ex-husband?!
Was he a good person? Was he compassionate? Was he driven by strong

personal instincts? Was he financially well-off? Was he driven by basic emotions, wanting to treat all those women in such a way?!
This is how his life, once connected to my friend's life, has now left its mark as an unresolved memory, lingering as a trace of that first Apple Island friend in my psyche.

Different Thoughts 2

It was the first time I met a Korean mom. After 100 days, I had been staying at home with my baby, but finally, I ventured out slowly on my own, for the first time in a while, near my house. It was at a quiet nail shop where I met the Korean mom for the first time.

"Are you Korean?

Are you a mom?"

It was a natural first greeting. Furthermore, as we talked, we found out that our two babies were born in the same year, and their birth months were just one month apart—April and May. Maybe that's why I felt an inexplicable sense of closeness and shared understanding.

I am someone who is very shy and tends to speak little. Perhaps sensing that, the Rai's mom approached me first. Everything felt natural, and there was no discomfort.

After that, I also met her husband. One day, Rai-mom suggested that since her husband was going to the Reebok Center to work out, I should come along. Rai-mom and I took our babies, loaded the strollers into Rai-dad's car, and went out for a stroll in Soho. While pushing the strollers and walking down the familiar streets of Soho, we stopped at an outdoor café, parked the strollers, and sat down. I covered my chest and shoulders with a small baby blanket to nurse, while Rai-mom fed her baby with a bottle. We shared various stories as we talked...

Rai-mom and I both had a quiet, cautious approach towards each other, and our personalities were similar, speaking softly to each other. We didn't engage much in the usual small talk or basic background questions. It was simply a comfortable, human conversation. Unexpectedly, we found we shared similar interests in art, museum visits, and volunteering. We also had the same thoughts about how, when our children grew older and no longer needed their mothers' hands, we would each return to the activities and pursuits we had wanted to do.

Rai's dad and my man would often meet, and they'd sometimes play poker with Rai-dad's friends. Rai-mom and I shared a quietly smooth relationship, like clouds slowly drifting by, living in a comfortable harmony.

Some weekends, we would visit Rai-mom's house in Bayonne, where she would invite us over for dinner. Rai-mom, who loved grapes and knew a lot about wine, would sometimes enjoy wine with me, and we'd spend some simple, quiet time together. Most of our gatherings were just casual, easy meetings with Rai-mom and the babies.

One day, Rai-mom told me she was planning to visit Korea and take a short trip to Jeju Island, but she hadn't decided on her return date yet. At the same time, I found myself in a situation where I had to suddenly relocate to California, and that's when we lost touch.

Years passed, and one day I saw Rai-mom on the internet. The articles and photos displayed were completely unimaginable for someone like her. She was in a relationship with a married public figure, and she had become the subject of public attention as his mistress. I couldn't believe it.

So much time had passed, and many circumstances had changed. I couldn't know the exact start or end of their story, but... I couldn't bring myself to read the article about Rai-mom to the end. I couldn't read it.

The first time I became a mother, and the first time I met this Korean mom, it all felt so naturally connected. But understanding this reality... this was now the life of that mom.

Different Thoughts 3

The first time I met the influencer-mom, I wasn't interested in influencers, nor did I know much about them. It was a field that had nothing to do with me. At my man's suggestion, I ended up co-hosting an exhibition in California with this influencer-mom and three foreign artists.

As expected, I have a shy personality, so I was quietly organizing my artwork and setting up the display, assisted by someone helping me. The influencer-mom approached me first, introduced herself, and with a shared bond of being a mother, she came closer to me. Her bold personality and natural talent for speaking made it clear that she could captivate anyone with her words, rather than just speaking fluently.

Once I finished setting up the display, I turned to my assistant and suggested that we prepare the artwork captions.
The influencer-mom came over and asked, "What's a caption?"
I thought I had misunderstood her, so I politely asked her to say again.
The influencer-mom repeated, "What's a caption?"
I hesitated for a moment and then answered, "Simply put, it's an introduction or name tag for the artwork. You place it next to each piece."

The influencer-mom asked me to lend her a caption for one of the artworks. I handed one to her. The influencer-mom then showed the sample caption to her two assistants and instructed them to quickly prepare captions for her own artworks. After finishing the preparations for the exhibition, I said my goodbyes to the other artists and was leaving the exhibition hall. The influencer-mom, happy to have another artist in the exhibition, invited me to dinner. I was caught off guard and couldn't respond immediately. The influencer-mom, being straightforward, reassured me that it was fine and asked me to get in touch later, handing me her business card.

After the exhibition was successfully concluded over the course of three days, I felt I should at least have a cup of coffee with the influencer-mom, so I set aside some time for it. The influencer-mom expressed her gratitude for the caption I had given her. Unexpectedly, we ended up talking for about an hour and a half.

From then on, despite being completely different in every way, the influencer-mom and I would call each other every year on our birthdays to check in. The influencer-mom would encourage me, urging me to step out into the world... I would just smile in response.

Before My Breath is Scattered

The influencer-mom has over 1 million followers. She has a personality that does whatever she wants. She is a woman with a strong sense of ownership, having everything she desires. There's no hesitation in her actions, and she loves to express herself with flair. Already famous and constantly striving to maintain and grow her fame, she is deeply driven by the desire to keep getting more recognition.

With high subscriber numbers and a substantial weekly income, this is her reality. To maintain it all, from the moment she wakes up in the morning until she closes her eyes at night, the camera is always rolling, capturing every moment of her day. She is constantly accompanied by her team, and she truly enjoys all of it—the filming, the attention, and the lifestyle that comes with it.

Suddenly, through a phone call, I received the news. Later, the influencer-mom boldly shared it on her social media. She had ended her marriage—a divorce. Life, as anyone can agree, is never perfect, and this is something that resonates with every human being.
I continued to see the influencer-mom's photos and updates being posted, and it was a strange feeling. She had once been the mom I first met through a shared bond of being fellow mothers, someone I connected with through a small exchange of information. Now, though living a

different life as a mother, and on the other side of the world, I hope for her life to continue peacefully. I sincerely wish that the life she longs for will come true, wherever she may be.

Different Thoughts 4

The first time I met this YouTuber, who was also a fellow mom, was through my man's shooting club meeting. She was known within the group as a wealthy woman, with both a child and a husband who was very financially successful. We had a few conversations, and after the club meeting ended, members sometimes shared a couple of drinks together at a wine lounge.

Most people came to the gatherings alone, and there were few couples like my man and I who attended together. On one occasion, after a meeting, we sat together for a while, and I noticed that she was sitting across from me, talking to a male member of the group. At one point, I saw her gently patting his back while talking to him. Some of the other members saw this but didn't seem to be bothered. I was puzzled at first—perhaps I was misreading the situation. Were they close? But I couldn't shake off the discomfort, especially since they were both married and the act seemed somewhat intimate, though not visibly drunk. The situation continued with her caressing his back in a way that could easily be misunderstood. I quietly told my man that we should leave, and we went home.

At the next meeting, she was interacting mainly with the men. Then, unexpectedly, she approached me and wanted to talk. It seemed like she wanted to address her behavior at the previous gathering. Since there weren't many moms in the group, I assumed she might have felt the need to clarify. She explained that her marriage had been arranged by her family, and that they had a premarital agreement that shaped their relationship. She said that she was living according to that agreement and doing what she wanted in her life. I apologized for previously staring, but she reassured me, saying it was fine, and that anyone in that situation could have noticed. Afterward, she returned to the group of men, raised her wine glass, and gestured to me to toast. I did the same in return.

Over time, I began to understand her behavior better, as it became clear that the other members knew about her life and accepted her actions. Her life was simply part of her story, and those around her weren't bothered by it. Eventually, we stopped attending the shooting club meetings and also stopped going to the pub or wine lounge gatherings.

After some time had passed, I found out through social media that that mom had become a YouTuber. She even sent me a friend request. With a congratulatory message, I accepted her request, and we became acquaintances.

A few years later, that mother became famous, a YouTuber with over 300,000 views. People complimented:

"The object of envy of other moms."

"A wife who is good at helping out."

"A mom who is good at raising children."

"A woman who has the everything." These were some of the words used to praise her.

Even at this moment, innumerable videos and YouTubers are being created. New content needs to be made continuously by countless people who search for and watch YouTube. It makes me realize that not just anyone can do it.

The first YouTuber I personally got to know—the mom who established her fame and is firmly in control. I hope she continues to live, enjoying the life she confidently approved of for herself.

MY LIFE:

A Freelancer is Not Free

Me - just a mommy, an ordinary human.

But in their eyes, I was easy prey.

- Kimisoo Kim

There is a Korean proverb: "배운 게 도둑질" (Baeun-ge dodukjil), which translates to, "What you learned is theft."

If you hear this proverb for the first time, you might feel uncomfortable due to the negative connotations of the word "theft" and this discomfort likely comes from the images this word conveys. However, when you think about its meaning, this proverb actually captures the essence of learning.

"Whatever you've learned becomes the path you walk."

This is the truth embedded in the saying.

Looking back on my life, there are many things I've learned and come to love.

One of these is Design.

The experiences I accumulated while studying, along with the talents I naturally developed over time,

all encompass Design. That's why I've never forgotten it for a moment—design is a part of my identity.

Writing is the same.

If design is about communicating with the world through visual language, then writing is another way of expressing the thoughts deep inside my heart.

Even after becoming a mother, design and writing never disappeared from my life.

Then, when my child started going to school, I found a bit of free time, and with that, I was able to freelance. I found a job through Glassdoor, sent my resume, interviewed, and started right away.

The owners ran a men's clothing business and were parents of daughters, which was a common bond between us, as I was also a mother of a daughter. However, there was no paperwork when I started, and many aspects of the job differed from my previous experiences.

From the beginning, I communicated via emails, especially for my compensation: basic details, the tasks I completed in the first week, and the dates and hours I worked. The boss instructed me to forward this information to another employee in charge, and I complied. After some time, despite working as a freelancer, I didn't receive any response about my pay. So, I sent another email to remind them of the points we discussed in the interview. However, their words and actions suddenly didn't align with anything before. They spoke to me in a negative tone, almost threatening.

Then what was the last day of work with them, I quietly saved all the work I had done on my laptop, said goodbye as usual, and left the company office. Later that evening, I emailed them to inquire about my wages, but their response was completely unreasonable—they said my work was totally useless and they cannot pay me anything!

There was a Freelancers Union who helped and advised me—there was no other way. Consequently, I decided I had to sue.

One day, while I was at Bloomingdale's in Soho, I found their label displayed in the Men's basement. Many of the pieces I had worked on were hanging there in the store, and they were exactly what I created! I was heartbroken.

The trial went in my favor since they didn't even show up, and I received court documents confirming my ruling. However, during the process of trying to enforce my judgement with those documents, I found changes in their business information. I went back to the court to explain the situation, informing them that the legal company name had changed, and so I filed a revision. Over time, I received additional court papers having to confirm that the legal company name had changed yet again. Through public records, I found that the company had been involved in numerous lawsuits. They were also continually changing their legal business name and address, yet still operating under the same brand. Even today, in New York City, their recorded company names are constantly changing: IsXXXXX Holdings, IsXXXXX LLC, IsXXXXX Inc, IsXXXXX-US, IsXXXXX... The names change endlessly.

Discovering The Outlaws

I read an article stating that *The Outlaws 2* was currently being screened in the U.S. Over the decades spent on Apple Island, I haven't had much exposure to Korean movies.

Other movies and thoughts that come up when I think of this are:

My Teacher, Mr. Kim
...I remember the purity of children.

1987: When the Day Comes
"When the investigator slammed the desk, he gasped and then collapsed."

For a while, I was heartbroken. For a while, I was angry. I express my deepest condolences to the precious sacrifices of the lives of so many college students and profound gratitude for the freedom regained by them.

Keys to the Heart
I think it's unnecessary to see being different as something different.
Being different is still an existence in itself. It's the preciousness of being together as a family.

I came to know about *The Outlaws 1* like this, and then I searched to watch it. After watching The Outlaws 1, the first emotion I felt was for the short but strong and meaningful lines of dialogue. The fact that the movie is based on a true story made me think that even though the details may have been adjusted for film, the reality of the events, involving the Wang Geon and Black Snake factions, felt even more brutal and surprising. Ultimately, the movie was about a fight for money and territory.

The second feeling I felt was from the portrayal of the powerful detective character. He was not the typical image of a detective one might expect. He wasn't the usual short-haired, tough-guy gangster type either. Instead, he had the physique of a superhero with an unpolished, raw way of speaking. The use of human and humorous expressions, which didn't seem to align with his tough image, was striking.

The final emotion I felt was regarding the tools used, commonly used in Western films, for the most part, guns. Personally, the gun I am interested in is the Non-NFA Maxim 9. In this film, however, it was the bare fists, steel pipes, chains, axes, and knives that were used as extensions and tools of violence. Because of this, you could see an emphasized grimness in the color tone, reflecting the brutality of the bloody battles. It gave me a sense of fear, especially when a savage scene approached, making me feel like I might have to cover my eyes with my hands to shield myself from what was to come. In an ironic moment, the detective character's humorous lines served to soften the brutal moments, almost as if turning the violence into a light watercolor, adding an unexpected nuance to the atmosphere.

The combination of brutal real-life events and humorous dialogue, along with each actor's strong and distinct character, was something I could feel in every performance. The fast-paced action and camera work captured the director's passion, and I could feel the director's enthusiasm for every shot.

Before My Breath is Scattered

This is a well-made film. I also saw a preview for *The Outlaws 3*, in which they battle the Yakuza. The rapid progression of events after the success of the previous film was clear. The word "Yakuza" suddenly brought up some very old memories.

When I visited Japan, I heard the police patrol during the day, but at night the Yakuza control the streets. It is impossible to estimate the proportion of the Korean in Yakuza. However, it is undeniable that a significant number of members and those in key positions are of Korean descent.
Among the cities I visited in Japan—Osaka, Tokyo, Kyoto—the concept of their

'nawabari' (territory) strikes my thoughts.

And I still cannot forget how I enjoyed drinking the hiresake (hot sake with Tiger Fugu fin). Thoughts of omotenashi (mindful attention) and hospitality also occurs to me.

From the moment I first held a brick phone in my hands to using an iPhone now, I reflect on the countless changes that have swept through my life and the passing of time marked by shifting landscapes. As a mother to my one and only daughter, in this unexpected reality shaped by an accident that has made it impossible to return to normalcy, I

Before My Breath is Scattered

quietly take a moment—just for today—to revisit the memories of the past.

And then, gently, I send them back to where they belong, far away, to their rightful place once more.

Abduction

One day, while watching the news, a moment I had long forgotten suddenly resurfaced.
The news article was about a kidnapping incident.
A heavy and fearful word seeped into the corner of my heart.
And an experience from long ago flashed into focus.

I was living in Manhattan in New York.
My friend and I were the same age and attended the same school.
Both of us enjoyed adventure, so a life that took risks wasn't unfamiliar to us.

Before My Breath is Scattered

After finishing our last school assignment, we headed to Saint Marks Place.

We took a taxi downtown and found a small restaurant called Taisho, famous for its yakitori.

At Taisho, my friend ordered beer, and I ordered sake.

We shared grilled skewers and slowly savored the evening.

We were friends who respected each other's inner selves without saying much, and perhaps because we had walked the same path together, we were able to share our hearts with some ease.

After finishing our meal, we stepped out onto the street to hail a taxi.

As we waited for a moment, a black boxy car pulled up in front of us.
Inside the car were four men, and they were staring at us silently.
In that moment, a wave of fear instinctively rushed over both of us.
I shouted, "Call the police!" and my friend desperately screamed out, "Help! Help!"
Our cries as two East Asian women caught the attention of those around us.
Then, as quickly as it came, the black car disappeared.
The fear I felt that moment still lingers vividly in my memory.
I can't even imagine what might have happened if my friend hadn't been there with me.

Before My Breath is Scattered

We didn't go to our respective homes; instead, we headed to a hotel near Times Square.

It was a place where the lights never went out, a 24-hour spot with tourists and people constantly coming and going.

That night, we had a deep conversation and got to know more about each other.

We discovered some unexpected commonalities.

We both had a rule: we never walked alone at night.

One of us was the daughter of a big shot, and the other was someone's precious person.

That incident brought us closer, but after graduation, we decided to go our separate ways.

Before My Breath is Scattered

After our last conversation at the coffee lounge of the Royalton Hotel, located at 44 West 44th Street in Manhattan, we erased each other's contact information. It was a bittersweet farewell, but it was the last time we would meet.

A few years later, I heard that my friend had become a professor in Korea.
I was relieved to hear that my friend was doing well.
We could have easily found each other if we wanted to, but it seems we both quietly decided to live our own lives. Though many years have passed and our faces have changed, I believe the story of that night will still remain in our memories.

Now, I live a life with a disability, but for my daughter, who keeps me breathing, I am preparing to step back into the world.

And I live on, burying the riddle of that night deep in a corner of my heart, as if I've forgotten it.

It remains a hanging mystery.

That night, who was it that the black car was looking for?

Returning

We have returned.

After six long years, our family has come back to Apple Island.

I didn't think it would take this long.

The moment we arrived at the airport, I felt relief wash over me.

My breath came so easily here.

The noise, the crowds of people, the towering buildings that seem to block out the sun—

I had missed it all dearly.

I had so longed for it.

And along with us, our cherished and meaningful memories have returned too.

Before My Breath is Scattered

They are the traces of the countless days and years my daughter and I spent at Barnes & Noble.

My three-year-old daughter, from such a young age, carefully chose and collected the books on her own.

Over time, her collection grew to 30 boxes.

These boxes of books are now packed among our moving crates,

and three weeks from now, they will be delivered to us—

to her.

Inside those boxes lie more than just books.

Before My Breath is Scattered

They hold the footsteps and memories of my daughter and me,
walking together over six years,
a mother afraid to drive and her little girl,
side by side.
These boxes are treasures,
holding the traces of a life we built,
one step at a time.

Our family coordinated my daughter's school registration to align with the date our belongings were to be transported and began, bit by bit, organizing and settling into the new condo we had secured in advance.

And so, life in the same old city—the life on Apple Island—began once more. It feels soft and warm, as though cradled by the clouds in the sky, bringing a gentle, cozy happiness. My daughter and I will continue to walk this path together, as always.

Before My Breath is Scattered

Why Do I Still Wear a Mask?

"One day, someone who had come across my writing asked me a curious question."

Since the start of the COVID-19 pandemic and throughout its prolonged, dangerous period, I began wearing a mask.
Even now, in 2024, I still don't take it off when I step outside.
Of course, there could be various assumptions.
Some might think I wear it because I lack confidence in my appearance, or because I feel it's better to show only my eyes.
Others might suggest it's a convenient tool for hiding skin troubles.

Before My Breath is Scattered

But the real reason I wear a mask is something only I know—
Something deeply personal to me.
My life... has it always been this way, where such things find their way to me?
It's because of the results of a failed orthodontic treatment.

At first, I didn't care much about orthodontics. When my mouth is closed and when my teeth are visible, I have entirely different faces.
These two faces make it feel as though two versions of me coexist.
Even at my wedding, there isn't a single photo of me laughing.
I simply kept my lips pressed together, offering a quiet smile.

I never thought it was a significant issue for me.

When speaking, I would always talk slowly or cover my mouth with my hand.

That's just how I lived.

As time passed following childbirth, I went for a routine dental check-up.

The dentist began recommending orthodontic treatment, explaining that my uneven teeth could lead to improper brushing, potentially harming my gums and overall dental health.

Those words made me pause and think.

Eventually, I decided to start orthodontic treatment later in life.

However, the results were different from what I had expected.

The orthodontist said that my facial bone structure and teeth were "stubborn," giving reasons that didn't quite make sense.

Whether it was a failure in the treatment plan or not, during the middle of the treatment process, without my consent, I was reassigned to another orthodontist. Moreover, although I had already paid the full treatment fee, due to incorrect medical procedures, the outcomes promised by the orthodontist were not carried out. They even handed me a second invoice of $5,947.50 to continue treatment.

Before My Breath is Scattered

From the beginning of all this, I make sure to wear a mask every time I go out. From that start, even with my life turned upside down by an unexpected car accident that left me with a disability, wearing a mask has continued to be part of my daily routine.

It's not just to cover my face.
It might also be because I don't want to make others uncomfortable.
When I wear a mask, there's a sense of relief as if my concerns don't get passed on to others.
Perhaps it's a bit of a cowardly feeling, but it's because I want to find some mental peace in the distance from others.

Living with a mask on, I stand in front of the mirror today and think.

If there's anyone out there, like me, who is considering orthodontics at a later age, I hope this writing can be of some help.

I express the hope that my story and experience might add a little more careful thought to your decision.

During the COVID-19 pandemic, masks became a natural part of daily life as anything else.

While keeping our distance from strangers, masks were shields protecting us, a kind of safety device.

Before My Breath is Scattered

As we walked down the streets, half-covering our faces, we unknowingly began living a new kind of daily life.

However, as time passed, this mask gradually started to come off people's faces.

As the situation slowly improved, it became possible to take off the masks, but I still wear mine.

Now, as fewer people wear masks and more people show their bright, smiling faces, I can't help but feel a little pang in my heart.

I don't know how long I will continue wearing my mask.

Still, now that this mask has become a part of my daily life, taking it off feels strangely unfamiliar.

Before My Breath is Scattered

Standing in front of people without a mask now feels odd, as if a part of me is disappearing.

The expression behind the mask has hidden the emotions I wished to conceal, becoming my small shield of protection.

But I hope the day will come soon when I have to take off that shield.

There will be a moment when I remove this thin piece of paper that has protected me and, eventually, blend in naturally with others.

Breakfast with the Mayor

Starting 20**, through my daughter's father, our family was invited to attend the annual Veterans Day breakfast at the residence of the Mayor of New York City. Veterans Day is a day to reflect on and honor the sacrifices, dedication, and spirit of the veterans who fought for peace in our nation and the world. It is a moment to express gratitude and respect for their patriotism and noble service, while also conveying our heartfelt appreciation for all they have given.

Each year, upon receiving the invitation, we enter the New York Mayor's residence only after undergoing a detailed identity check, followed by two rounds of rigorous security screening. Everywhere, we see countless security personnel stationed, their presence more palpable in real life than any scene from a movie. Since it's a breakfast event, even the chefs and staff preparing the food wear transparent earpieces. Everyone, dressed in their respective uniforms, has these earpieces in one ear, badges on display, and even holstered firearms visibly integrated into their attire. They stand attentively in their designated positions.

My daughter greets the security guards, and some even give her a cheerful high-five. They speak to her kindly, ensuring she feels at ease, offering her warm and gentle interactions. After the breakfast concludes, our family follows the guidance of the staff to move to the adjacent hall, where the next part of the event, the Mayor of New York's speech, is set to take place.

Inside the venue, journalists, broadcast reporters, cameras, and various media personnel are stationed, waiting in their designated areas. Alongside Navy, Air Force, Army, and Marine Corps personnel, there are also soldiers from other affiliations present. Our family, starting with introductions to the generals, gradually exchanged greetings with soldiers from different branches, as well as veterans and other invited guests.

Before I realized it, tears began to stream down my face. I felt an overwhelming desire to express my gratitude and appreciation once more. Among them were veterans who had served in the Korean and Vietnam Wars. One of the veterans approached our family and asked which country we were from. Suddenly, my daughter answered, "We're Korean." For a moment, the veteran reminisced, sharing memories of their time during the Korean and Vietnam Wars. My man shares his thoughts, "Thank you for your service. It's an honor sir."

Seeing them brought me to a moment of deep reflection as a Korean, a moment to renew my gratitude for the veterans and the Korean Armed Forces. Like the U.S. Veterans Day, it reminded me of Korea's Armed Forces Day on October 1st, a day to honor and remember their sacrifices and contributions.

After the event concluded, we returned home. As a family, we decided to make a small contribution of our own. We resolved to prepare poppy flower brooches for the following year. The poppy, a symbol of remembrance for soldiers who gave their lives on the battlefield, continues to be a meaningful tradition observed worldwide on Veterans Day. With this spirit, the three of us spent a week assembling 1,000 poppy brooches, piecing them together one by one.

In 20**, we were re-invited to the New York Mayor's residence for the Veterans Day breakfast. After the meal, we headed to the starting point of the parade. There, with gratitude in our hearts, we distributed the 1,000 poppy brooches to those participating in and organizing the parade. It may not have been much, but it was a heartfelt gesture of appreciation. For our family, it was an incredibly moving and proud moment, one that brought tears to our eyes.

Even then, we couldn't have imagined what other moments the future might hold for us.

First Accident

One weekend, we were driving to another island for my man and daughter's air rifle practice. On the Long Island Expressway, the car in front of the car ahead of us suddenly stopped, but there was enough distance between the car ahead and us to stop with a gap to spare.

But how many seconds had passed? Our car, which was standing still, was suddenly struck in a violent collision from behind. The car behind us, without slowing down, rammed into us full force. I was seated in the rear-right seat, and in that moment of impact, my breath was completely stolen away. There was no screeching of brakes, no warning at all. What was that driver even doing? In the split second of impact, my seatbelt tightened sharply, holding me in place so firmly that I couldn't even breathe.

My man, sitting in the driver's seat, briefly lost consciousness, and I, struggling to regain my bearings, kept speaking to my daughter, who was sitting in the front seat, trying to keep her calm. The car's road service SOS signal automatically activated, and a voice began to speak. Our car was a brand-new German SUV. In that moment, the vehicle we were in had instantly transformed into a completely totaled car.

A few minutes later, three fire trucks and four police cars arrived, taking over the road, while sand was spread across the pavement. Five ambulances also arrived with sirens blaring. It was a major accident. Our family was loaded into two different ambulances and taken to the emergency room, the sound of sirens accompanying us, as if the noise itself was signaling the start of a new chapter in our lives.

When we arrived at the emergency room, we were all instructed by the nurses to separate for various exams. I wanted to stay with my daughter. The nurse brought me two sheets of paper and asked for my signature. It stated that I agreed to delay my own examination, understanding the decision, and taking responsibility for it. So, I stayed by my daughter's side while she underwent her tests.
Ten hours later, we left the emergency room and took a car-service home. Following the emergency room doctor's recommendation, our family returned to

the hospital the next day for further detailed tests.

Months later, very suddenly, I began to experience symptoms of pain. I couldn't sit. I couldn't stand. My body and mind were overwhelmed by pain and agony, as if my entire being was being consumed. My body trembled uncontrollably like from an electric shock, and it felt as though my bones were scraping against each other. I took strong painkillers. I received strong pain injections. But nothing helped. At least when I lay down, it was somewhat more bearable.

At another doctor's, as I slowly regulated my breathing while lying down, tears flowed uncontrollably because of the pain that started. The pain was so intense that, even after receiving powerful painkillers, it didn't subside. They applied an ice pack and, after an hour, received another pain injection. Still, the pain didn't leave me.

With much assistance I returned home. There were eight different new medications prescribed to me. It felt like I was going to die. I also felt so unjustly wronged. My presence felt like it was slipping away. I felt so weak and just wanted to give up.
The day stretched on endlessly, feeling unbearably long. I could only do things while lying down—using the bathroom,

eating, drinking water, even holding my daughter—all while lying down. There was nothing I could do other than lie down. And all the pain and suffering remained with me.

Even with the close care of my man and daughter, they couldn't reach me through the pain, irritation, anger, and suffering that surrounded me. I couldn't see the gratitude.

I was trapped on the edge of a cliff, unable to escape the inevitable pain and fear, only wanting to avoid it, shuddering. There was only the feeling of wanting to give up before even starting. I tried desperately to be strong, to accept things positively. I knew I had to accept the reality, coldly and fairly, that I could never return to how I was... I had no choice but to accept and endure it, and this emotional rollercoaster repeated itself. To come to terms with the reality that I could never return to normal, I kept repeating the present reflection.

The pain felt as if my bones were being scraped, like they were cutting into each other, and I screamed, soaked in tears and sweat, in agony...
My one and only daughter who was watching me, the only one who could give me breath, I felt so sorry to her. I felt so

regretful. My heart was broken and seared.

I could feel the truth of the saying that life doesn't allow us to see clearer even an inch ahead. With that, I briefly entertained the thought that maybe, just maybe, a moment of joy could come, even though I couldn't see it. Nonetheless I kept promising myself, again and again, that I had to accept and acknowledge the reality that I could never return to how I was.

It was the beginning of an endless series of painful moments. It might take a long time. The outcome was uncertain.

So on Apple Island, began the treatments for Mommy Papillon.

Before My Breath is Scattered

Pee Pads

Pain arrived without warning.

After the car accident, agony engulfed my entire body.

I couldn't move, couldn't even take a step.

It was as though I had regressed to infancy—

even crawling on my stomach was impossible.

Only me and my daughter were left in our home.

I was trapped in confusion and pain, confined to a reality where I could barely catch my breath while lying down.

Then, out of nowhere, an urgent physiological need arose.

I had to use the bathroom, but I couldn't do a thing. In that moment, the urine simply flowed out of me. Tears flowed along with it.

I prayed my daughter wouldn't see, wouldn't be frightened. But she saw everything. My daughter immediately approached me and said,
"Mom, are you alright?"
I couldn't say anything or do anything. I could only lie there, soaked and ashamed.

Through the urinous smell, she said "Mom, it's okay. You just had an accident. You didn't have time to get to the bathroom." But my daughter didn't stop there. With her tiny hands, she began to help me as best as she could. She brought a towel and gently laid it beside me.

I said nervously, "This is 'ji-ji!' Mommy will clean it slowly."

But my daughter said, "Mom, it's okay! Just a moment."

Unable to move, all I could do was listen to the sounds, "Rustle, rustle..."

Moments later, she returned holding a fresh puppy pee pad. With her little hands, she struggled this way and that but managed to start to carefully slide it under me.

"Mom, you can pee on this. It's okay. I'll clean it up just like I do for our dog Toto."

As I witnessed this scene, my heart ached.

In my helplessness of not being able to do anything, my daughter, at her young age, was doing the best she could.

She showed me her love and caring.

Her warmth and thoughtfulness, shown through her tiny hands, momentarily enveloped me and eased my pain.

I laid there, saying nothing, thinking nothing, simply still.

Before My Breath is Scattered

This feeling—what I experienced at that moment—was perhaps the deepest connection one could feel as a human being, or more precisely, as a mother.
Though my daughter had witnessed my vulnerability for the first time, her small hands, filled with care and love, displayed strength greater than anything else.
As a mother, I had always thought of myself as the one who cared for my child, but in that moment, her actions gave me the will to keep going, and revealed the boundless depth of love.

That day, I could feel (human?) that the love between parents and children can rebuild a life with just one small,

Before My Breath is Scattered

heartfelt touch. And that there is something to learn...

Lingering at a Shopping Mall

After completing a regular hospital check-up, with my body still uncomfortable after the accident, I made a brief stop at the mall. Parking in a handicapped space, receiving support on one side, and holding a cane in the other, I slowly made my way inside. The automatic doors opened, parting to reveal what felt like an entrance to another world. The instant the cool blast of air-conditioning touched my skin, I felt both alive and acutely aware of the lingering numbness in parts of my body—a stark reminder of my current reality. A massive shopping mall, a marvel of modern civilization...

Inside, the shops were neatly aligned, yet what drew me in more than the opulent luxury brands was the sheer beauty of the space itself—a creation born of human ingenuity and craftsmanship. I don't chase after grandeur, but in this space, I wanted to feel something special. This wasn't merely a place to buy things—it was a space overflowing with the tangible results of human creativity and capability, and I sought to find my own sense of awe within it. Sunlight streamed through the vast glass ceilings, illuminating each shop in turn, its glow enhancing the carefully arranged displays of colors and textures. The harmony of hues and patterns, combined with the underlying hum of voices and footsteps, made the entire space feel like a living, breathing work of art. I paused for a moment, letting the emotions evoked by everything I saw seep deeply into me. I wanted to capture the vibrant energy of this place, unsure of when I might have the chance to return. Lifting my phone, I sought to memorialize this harmony of colors and arrangements, imprinting the emotions I felt during my brief time here into each photo I took. And so, for a short while, I remained amidst the tangible results of modern civilization. This was not just a shopping space—it was a testament to human creativity, leaving a profound impression on me. Even as I eventually left this place, the beauty I captured in

Before My Breath is Scattered

my photos will linger in my heart for a long time to come.

Before My Breath is Scattered

Before My Breath is Scattered

The Last Makeup

One day, I suddenly realized something.
Two surgeries, the deep and heavy slumber of anesthesia, the potent painkillers, and treatments—
these had left behind not only traces of physical pain.
They had etched profound anguish and torment within me,
and I began to gradually recognize those changes.

After the accident, I stopped wearing makeup.
No, it wasn't just that I stopped.
It felt as though the very act of wearing makeup had been lost from my life.

Before My Breath is Scattered

Even before the accident, makeup hadn't been a significant part of my daily routine.

A few small brown bottles were neatly placed on the cabinet near the bathtub—one toner, one moisturizer, and that was all.

In the drawer, there was an eyeliner pencil, a ChapStick, and an eyeshadow.

I couldn't even remember why or how they had ended up there.

Perhaps someone had left them behind.

Or maybe they were a fragment of a memory I had lost.

Every time I went to the hospital, I felt a desire to present myself neatly.

But I couldn't do anything.

Before My Breath is Scattered

Standing in front of the mirror, I thought about drawing my eyebrows, but my hands wouldn't move.

Whenever I tried to pick up the eyeliner pencil, a strange and uncomfortable sensation crept into my fingertips.

In the end, I put the pencil down.

I did nothing.

No, maybe I just didn't want to do anything.

Why? It felt as if I had forgotten how to put on makeup.

Surprisingly, that didn't sadden me.

Because I no longer felt the need for makeup.

Perhaps it was because I was always wearing a mask.

But then, a day came when I had to wear makeup.

A fundraising dinner for scholarships for children of fallen soldiers.

An event attended by notable and respected figures.

For that day, I genuinely wanted to give my best effort and participate.

My man booked a salon through Google Maps,

and after much hesitation, I opened the salon door and with help, stepped inside.

For the first time since my marriage, for the first and last time since the accident,

I spent two hours at the salon getting my makeup done.

Before My Breath is Scattered

The face in the mirror felt unfamiliar yet special.

For the first time in ages, I removed my mask and arrived at the dinner venue.

For three hours, I sat there as fatigue and discomfort washed over me,

but I stayed until the very end.

That day, I wanted to share my gratitude with everyone.

I think back to the face I saw that day.

I think back to who I was that day.

And I think of who I am today.

It reminds me that I endured, and that I am still alive.

Before My Breath is Scattered

Since

Things I Can Do Laying Down

After the accident, most of my life has been spent lying down.

I try to write. It's my desire to write down the thoughts that keep surfacing in my thoughts. I want to sit in a chair despite the pain, but I can't. The pain is unbearable. Even the strong painkillers prescribed by the doctor do not help. I find no value in life as I once knew it, and now, through this pain, I've come to realize the importance of a normal life, something I had been ignorant of before. It's only now that I understand the significance of something as seemingly trivial as sitting in a chair. In the end, there's nothing else I can do but lie down.

As I slowly take a deep breath in my horizontal position, the white ceiling comes naturally into view. A long, rectangular white ceiling. For some reason, tears start to flow. I find myself staring blankly, not to a burning campfire, but at this flat ceiling. The hardest part isn't the physical pain but the mental agony of accepting that I may never return to normal. It's difficult to fight this despair. Slowly I try to collect myself.

Before My Breath is Scattered

I must have dozed off for a moment. I woke up breathing calmly. Slowly, some words began to form in my mind. I immediately wrote them down. This is how lying down became a way for me to write.

As my treatment began with unpredictable results, after my first surgery, I am now waiting for the day when the second surgery will be scheduled, still mostly lying down. One day, unexpectedly, I tuned into a Korean radio channel and heard an advertisement. It was definitely English expressed in Korean words.

Is it the peculiar charm of Hangul? It evoked a strange feeling within me, one I wish to share.

Before My Breath is Scattered

So, I express it through writing:

Hangul: 운명의 데스티니

Romanization: unmyeong-ui deseutini

English: The destiny of fate

Hangul: 죽음의 데스

Romanization: jugeum-ui deseu

English: Death of the end

Hangul: 어둠의 다크

Romanization: eodum-ui dakeu

English: The dark of blackness

Hangul: 전설의 레전드

Romanization: jeonseol-ui lejeondeu

English: Legends of lore

Before My Breath is Scattered

Hangul: 원조의 오리지널

Romanization: wonjo-ui orijineol

English: Genuine original

Hangul: 소리의 사운드

Romanization: sori-ui saundeu

English: The sound of resonance

Hangul: 혼돈의 카오스

Romanization: hondon-ui kaoseu

English: The turmoil of chaos

Hangul: 다양한 버라이어티

Romanization: dayanghan beoraieoti

English: The variety of diversity

Before My Breath is Scattered

For someone unfamiliar with English, these could be interpreted as two different words. For someone who knows English, it's merely a repetition of the same term.

Yet the combination of the Hangul word and its English pronunciation feels so natural and deeply emotional. Hangul has such a rich array of sounds and expressions that they are often untranslatable into English. It's a uniquely diverse and vibrant language.

The greatness of Hangul, created by King Sejong and the scholars of the Hall of Worthies or 집현전 (Jiphyeonjeon), is evident in the records of its invention, its principles (like combining consonants and vowels, separating them, double consonants, diphthongs, etc.), and its purpose of making literacy accessible to the common people. This history remains intact even today. Is there any other native script in the world with such comprehensive documentation?

Living abroad, I took the idea of Hangul as my native language for granted. But now I realize that Hangul is a treasure, a beautiful cultural heritage of South Korea.

Recognizing the importance of my mother tongue, I taught Hangul to my daughter. She looks at "ㅇ" and says it's a circle, looks at "□" and says it's a square.

This is how circles and squares form letters. Even I feel as though I'm discovering this for the first time.

In the U.S., they call one's native language the "mother tongue." It's the language that enables communication with one's mother, a fundamental aspect of being human.

As Koreans, remembering the importance of our language on Hangul Day on October 9th and honoring our native script feels like a basic courtesy to our ancestors.

It Hurts More Because It's in Korean

It was the day for my spinal injection as scheduled by the doctor.

Even now, they hurt so much, I hate injections.

The nurses tell me, "Time heals all wounds." But from my experience, medicine is just bitter. Even now, I hate the medicine.

After the appointment, I went to H-Mart, a Korean supermarket, for the first time in a long while.

With the assistance of a cane, I slowly began to look around.

The store was packed with countless items, filled with such a diverse range of goods that it gave me a sense of Korean essence, as if the entire country had been condensed and brought here. The food and side dishes were so varied. Among them, the packaged tteok-bokki stood out clearly.

Seeing and feeling everything, my body couldn't handle it. I was already exhausted. Disappointed, I decided to stop here.

Before My Breath is Scattered

I stood in line to pay for some items I picked. When it was my turn, I walked slowly to the cashier. With assistance, I must have walked too slowly. The person standing behind me seemed impatient. I heard a whisper, soft like breathing, from the person behind me.

"ㅂㅅ 같은 게 집에나 있지!"

(Idiot... Why don't you stay home!) In that moment, I wanted to turn around. But then, a tear fell from my eye and rolled into my mask. It hurt. It really hurt. It hurt more because it was in Korean.

When I returned home, I took the prescribed medicine and lay down. I fell asleep immediately. The next morning arrived. The pain still lingered. But I could feel it. I could see it. My daughter had placed her cherished horse doll beside my face while she slept.

I thought again:
    "That person was the idiot...
    I am not an idiot...
    The truth is, I am disabled."

As long as my daughter, who helps me breathe, is with me, that fact will never change.

Signing to Stay Alive

It was the day of my first surgery.

I woke up around 6 a.m. without any thoughts.

I didn't want to think about anything.

Two hours later, at 8 a.m., I was scheduled to take the hospital's car to the medical center.

After arriving at the hospital, I was helped to a wheelchair and taken to a preparation room.

Preparations for surgery began. Three nurses entered my room.

They each took their roles, and one nurse brought in some papers. Together, she explained.

I had decided to undergo surgery because of the pain, the suffering, to stay alive.

I had to.

Yet at this moment, I suddenly felt like I had become deaf, blocked by fear and dread.

What if I die?

What if I lose my mind?

What if I never wake up, like a vegetable?

Since there's always a possibility of complications during surgery, the form required my consent, acknowledging the risks. I couldn't refuse to sign this acceptance,

It was a signature for a surgery in order to survive, a consent form for a surgery that could mean my death.

Only I could make this decision, a choice that I could only do and accept. The consequences would also be mine alone to bear.

I signed the form, and 30 minutes later, I was wheeled into the operating room. I saw magnificent machines. Seven or eight people in scrubs. The head spinal surgeon approached and said the procedure would begin, at the same time, anesthesiologist began speaking and I fell asleep.

Six hours later, I slowly wake up, still breathing. My consciousness is clearing. But my life ahead may not be the same as before.

My body may never return to its former normal state.

But I was still alive.

And soon, a date for my second surgery would be set.

Then, 30 minutes before entering the operating room, I would again be handed a consent form to sign—to stay alive.

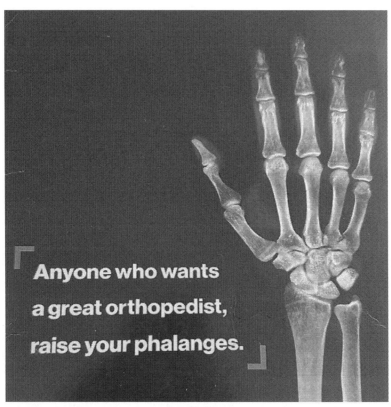

Afterwards

Do everything you want to do.

I am still afraid of injections. Typically, when receiving a spinal injection, the area is numbed with local anesthesia. The doctor uses a mobile X-ray machine called a C-arm during the procedure. Though the injections still scare me, this imposing machine now feels oddly familiar, almost like a friendly robot. After the injection, I lie down and rest for about 20 minutes before heading home.

During the week, as prescribed, I also receive acupuncture. The needles are about the length of my hand. The doctor knows how terrified I am just at the sight of them, so they always keep the needles hidden until the moment they're applied.

Following the prescription, I go to physical therapy two to three times a week. On days when the pain is particularly severe, the therapist has to roll me over, lift me, and help me move. If I suddenly experience a muscle cramp in my legs during therapy, it only makes things worse.

For one month, I stayed in bed at first, unable to do much else. And this has been my life for the past four years. About three to four times a year, I receive spinal injections. Most are administered near the tailbone, but today was the first time I received one in the lower left side of my back. After returning home, utterly exhausted, I lay down to rest.

Then, I received a message.
    "Do everything you want to do.
    I hope you will."
The sender, someone who had read my writings, must have sent it out of kindness and thoughtfulness.
In that moment, one thought filled my mind—what I truly want is to witness the growth of the one who gives me breath: my daughter.

"Do everything you want to do."
I read the message again, letting it sink in.

"Do everything you want to do."
What do I want to do? How can I make it happen? The message stirred these questions in me.

But what if I want to, yet time doesn't allow it?
What if I don't have the financial means?
What if my body fails me?
Am I taking this too seriously?

"Small but certain happiness."

—If it's small enough, wouldn't that make it easier to do everything I want? I let my imagination wander, indulging in my own thoughts.

Before My Breath is Scattered

Dreams exist because they can be dreamt.

Today is another day spent lying down.
As I stare at the ceiling, my eyes wander to the flower basket placed on the table.
In America, there is Father's Day and Mother's Day.
Today is Mother's Day.
I could feel it naturally.
In this moment, in this room, it is just me lying here, the flower basket that keeps me company, and the quiet air.
It is only silent.
Suddenly, I realize that, in my life so far, I've merely listened to the sounds that reached me from beyond my ears.
But here, alone in this room, I could hear the sounds within myself.

Before My Breath is Scattered

I attempt to listen to the moment of confronting this version of myself, lying here.

As a mother, I believe dreams exist because they can be dreamt.
As a mother,
Even if I am confined to lying down,
Even if I cannot move,
Even if all I have are thoughts,
Even if my wishes remain hopes,
Even if they are too grand,
Or perhaps a bit childish,
Dreams exist because they can be dreamt.

As a mother,
Even if I am too busy,
Even if I am too tired,

Before My Breath is Scattered

Even if I am lonely at times,

Even if I feel upset at times,

Even if no one understands me,

Even if the weather is too cold,

Even if the weather is too hot,

Dreams exist because they can be dreamt.

As a mother,

Even while holding a baby on my back and eating standing up,

Even while holding a baby on my back and doing the dishes,

Even while playing my "dishwashing drama" in the background

And pushing the vacuum,

Even while spending the whole day pushing a stroller around,

Dreams exist because they can be dreamt.

Before My Breath is Scattered

As a mother,

Dreams are simply meant to be dreamt.

Dreams are gifts that only I can give to myself.

Dreams are fleeting moments of joy for me.

Dreams bring a fleeting smile to my face.

Dreams are something only I can feel—

A spare piece of happiness, just for me.

As a mother,

Even if I were to spend the rest of my life lying down,

Dreams exist because they can be dreamt.

A Human Water Drop

For nearly a month, I couldn't go to the hospital for treatment and stayed confined to my bed at home. I couldn't even write.

Part of my body remains paralyzed, and though I want to walk, my leg often cramps and stiffens, making it hard to go outside.

Sometimes, when I look at my stiffened leg, it reminds me of dried pollack—its appearance dry and brittle, its touch hard and unyielding. In those moments, the sadness feels unbearable, yet I've endured such moments so many times that I sometimes feel hollow and numb.

My leg has grown weaker, even less reliable. To aid my walking, I was prescribed a new pair of forearm crutches, which I now use. My white cane, once a constant companion, now rests in my closet.

Today was a day for treatment. The appointments often involve nerve root injections or spinal facet joint injections, administered according to the doctor's judgment each time.
Today, under local anesthesia, I received a spinal injection in my pelvic bone.

Before My Breath is Scattered

Despite the anesthetic, I could still feel the pain, and it was agonizing. When I returned home, I collapsed into bed, drained. The lingering ache was so intense that human tears kept flowing.

> Human Water Drops
> Pain gathers.
> Agony approaches.
> Time passes.
> And then,
> When tears fill to the brim and overflow,
> They fall slowly from my eyes.
> The sobs accompany them gently down.
> Until every tear is spent, I wait.
> My voice bids them goodbye.
> My hand clutches a white tissue,

Before My Breath is Scattered

And collect the traces of tears.

Then,

My mind and heart give

Their final farewell.

As I lay there, tears streaming, I must

have fallen asleep.

A faint noise stirred me awake.

It was my daughter, back from school.

She kissed my cheek as I lay there.

It felt so warm.

It felt so peaceful.

And then, in her small voice,

"Hi, Mommy..."

The only thing I can do is write.

Since realizing I can never return to what I once considered "normal," I've made a conscious effort not to lose myself. From my bed, I searched for something I could still do, and that's when I stumbled upon a Korean writing platform.

Back in 2013, I had already published my first book sold at Barnes & Noble in New York, but this discovery brought a different kind of excitement. Writing in Korean and being acknowledged as an author through a pen name awakened a quiet thrill within me. It was a new beginning, one that continues to shape my journey today, as I take every opportunity to write. For me, this online medium has become a space of connection within my life spent lying down. It reminds me that humans are inherently social beings.

Though my writing may lack finesse, I've begun creating profusely in Korean. Amidst surgeries, endless treatments, injections, and the numbing haze of painkillers, a recurring fear often gripped me: "What if I lose my ability to write someday?" That thought, born from the fragility of my body and slowed reason, terrified me. But the more the fear grew, the harder I fought to stay present, to keep going. And because of that fear, I've held on tightly, refusing to let go, dragging myself forward to this very moment. To survive, perhaps even more than that—to live. Above all, for my daughter.

After what felt like an eternity of hesitation, I finally began preparing to step back out into the world. Though the door hasn't fully opened yet, I have started to pour my story into it, slowly and deliberately.

As I write, one thought lingers in my heart: "Just one more thing before leaving..."

Before My Breath is Scattered

Dear You,

To You, who may be crying alone at this very moment:

    "You are stronger than you think. This is not the time to break!"

To You, weighed down by a day filled with regret:

    "Regret is just another name for a new beginning!"

To You, standing at the edge of surrender:

    "It's too soon to give up!"

Before My Breath is Scattered

To You, who feels like everything has come to an end:

"Now is the perfect time to start again."

At this moment, somewhere out there, someone may be sitting with their head bowed low, wrestling with their pain in solitude. To them, I offer this small piece of my story, hoping it might bring even the faintest glimmer of comfort. May it create a stopgap for their breath, a moment to pause and gather strength.

And with this hope in my heart, I will knock on the door of the world once more.

The Days Spent Lying Down During the Pandemic

After the car accident, the pain that engulfed me was like an endless abyss of darkness.
Every day was a battle against pain.
It felt like a fight I could never win, leaving me helplessly lying there, powerless.

I had to spend day by day lying down.
Even basic needs—eating, drinking, using the restroom—had to be managed while lying down.
For the first time, I understood how one's body could feel like a heavy shackle.

Before My Breath is Scattered

Every moment was torment. But there was no other choice.

I could do nothing but remain lying down. The unique circumstances of the pandemic made enduring this pain even harder. Booking appointments and seeing doctors became a near-impossible task.
But by some stroke of luck, I managed to secure an appointment.
I lay in the backseat of the car with a pillow beneath me, and that's how I made my way to the hospital. Upon arrival, I was supported on both sides, barely able to make it inside.
Unable to sit due to the excruciating pain, I lay on a makeshift bed in the hospital, waiting for my turn.

Before My Breath is Scattered

When I finally saw the doctor, they administered an injection into my spine based on the MRI results.

Twenty minutes later, the doctor checked my condition again, but the pain remained unchanged.

Sweat poured down my face, tears streamed from my eyes, and even snot ran uncontrollably.

The pain showed no signs of easing, and I ended up receiving another pain relief injection.

But even after waiting another twenty minutes, nothing changed.

The pain dug deeper, sharper into my body.

The doctor eventually recommended surgery, scheduling it for a week later.
I was helped into the car to return home, but as the pain intensified, uncontrollable screams flew out of my lips.
Even the agony of childbirth seemed insignificant compared to this torment.

Eventually, I passed out in the car.
How much time had passed?
When I opened my eyes, I found myself lying in my room at home.
For a brief moment, a sense of peace, like heaven itself, washed over me, a stark contrast to the hellish pain.
Simply lying there was the only way to momentarily escape this relentless agony.

Before My Breath is Scattered

As I lay there, I slowly turned my head to the side.

My daughter was quietly watching me.

The thought of how much of a burden I had become to her, how much heartbreak I must be causing her, suffocated me with guilt.

Yet, I made a resolution.

For the sake of my daughter, I would endure all of this pain.

I promised myself I would withstand this long and grueling battle until the very end.

Even now, as the pain remains my constant companion, I have chosen not to let go of hope.

Before My Breath is Scattered

I believe that if I can overcome this pain, a day will surely come when I can walk side by side with my daughter again.

Courage on the Ground

In the long tunnel of the pandemic, we all experienced our routines closing in, our lives changing, and the world becoming unbearably difficult.
This shift did not spare me either. Especially when I crossed the threshold of the hospital, burdened by excruciating pain, it felt like the suffering was no longer just my own.

That day, following the doctor's instructions, I went for an MRI.
Standing was out of the question, and even sitting was impossible.

Before My Breath is Scattered

Supported by my man, I lay across the backseat of the car as we headed to the hospital.

We arrived at Lenox Hill Radiology.

From the moment I reached the hospital entrance, I couldn't take a single step without someone's help.

With a nurse assisting us, my man helped me into the waiting area.

But I couldn't sit down.

Leaning on a cane, I pressed my trembling body against the wall, barely able to remain upright.

While my man stepped away briefly to confirm our appointment, the pain began to crush me more and more.

It was so unbearable that I could barely breathe.

In that moment, there was only one thing I could do—

I had to lie down.

Slowly, I lowered myself to the ground. Thankfully, the waiting area was empty. As soon as my body met the cold floor, I was finally able to catch my breath.

That brief reprieve didn't last long. My man returned, and without even enough time to register his startled expression at seeing me sprawled on the ground, a male nurse came rushing over.

"I saw it on the camera and thought you might have collapsed," he said, his voice thick with concern.

Before My Breath is Scattered

My man explained the situation, and the nurse, now reassured, helped lift me and carried me to the MRI preparation room.

Even as I changed into a hospital gown, lying down the entire time, my man stayed close, assisting me.

Then, with the nurse's help again, I was transferred to the MRI room.

The scan lasted nearly two hours.

During that time, trapped in the deafening noise of the machine, unable to move, I endured yet another layer of torment.

When the scan finally ended, I still couldn't move on my own.

The male nurse once again lifted me and brought me to the changing room, where my man helped me get dressed.

And then, with the nurse's assistance once more, I was carried back to the car's backseat.

I thanked him countless times before we left.

At home, as I laid my weary body on the bed, a thought occurs to me.

For the first time in my life, I had lain down on the floor of a public space without any hesitation.

"Was that courage?"

"Was it a peculiar kind of confidence, knowing that avoiding the pain was impossible, so I chose to face it head-on?"

"Or was it an instinctive refusal to let the pain dominate me, a way of protecting my body and spirit?"

On that floor, in that moment…

NOW:

I Am Trying Not to Rely on Tranquilizers

In life, there are moments when one comes close to the threshold of death.

I have faced such moments.

Each time, the fragility and inevitability of life linger quietly in a corner of my heart.

In those moments, I've realized how precious it is to breathe and how fragile the thread of life truly is—a truth that has sincerely imprinted itself upon me.

The Threat in Manhattan

A while back, as I was leaving a restroom at a place called New Yorking, a stranger suddenly pointed a gun at me.

Before My Breath is Scattered

My vision spun, and my body, as if frozen, could not move.

Looking down the barrel of the gun, I witnessed the person's eyes were emotionless, and for a moment, it felt as though all sound had disappeared.

In that brief moment, a torrent of thoughts rushed at me.

All I had done was step out of a restroom, and now my life could suddenly end here.

Fortunately, his hand slowly lowered. Then, his group approached. I will never know what he thought or why he changed his direction, but after they left, I carefully and cautiously made my way out of that place.

The Nightmare on the Highway

It happened on the highway.

My man was driving us home as I sat in the passenger seat beside him.

Suddenly, a motorcycle gang of over 50 bikes swarmed our car.

They roared their engines loudly, speeding dangerously close to us.

Neither my man nor I could understand their intentions, but we had no choice except to follow their taillights.

For a full 30 minutes, we were forced to match their speed, compelled to keep driving, as I prayed desperately for the ordeal to end safely.

Throughout that time, worst-case scenarios raced through my heart as we helplessly navigated among their group, searching for a way to escape.

Then, as abruptly as they appeared, they changed direction and vanished.

I could finally catch my breath.

In that moment, I felt a deep pain in my chest, as though my heart itself had borne the strain...

The Miracle in Subzero Weather

One wintry day during my pregnancy, as I was walking slowly along a snow-covered path, my body suddenly gave out, and I collapsed to the ground.

Like a fallen leaf, I gently sank to the earth.

The cold air wrapped around me as the chill of the ground seeped through my entire body, and in that moment, it felt as though my body and mind were no longer my own.

The soft sound of falling snow mingled with the faint murmurs around me until all noise seemed to fade into silence. Thankfully, some strangers came to my aid, and with their helping hearts, I was soon safely transported to the emergency room.

In that moment, I deeply felt the fragility of life, fearful until the ER doctor finally assured me that the baby inside me was unharmed. I then truly understood what it meant to breathe a sigh of relief.

The German Car Mishap

It happened on Edgewater Road—this perilous incident.

We were riding in our meticulously repaired German car, one we had trusted for its safety, when strange noises began to emerge.

Inside the car, the sound of parts breaking off grew loud and a sudden powerful "thunk" dropped from behind. The vehicle swayed erratically, dragging itself along the road, and the steering wheel became uncontrollable.

In that moment, every cell in my body was overcome with despair and fear.

With the hazard lights on, my man struggled to steer us toward the shoulder of the road.

After several tense attempts, he managed to bring the car to a stop.

Without hesitation, he retrieved a portable oxygen can and handed it to me, speaking words of reassurance.

Bystanders who had witnessed the incident approached, offering their help.

Soon, police cars arrived at the scene.

I was so glad we didn't get on the GW...

The Collision on the Road

While heading to the shooting range on LIE 495, we were suddenly caught in a traffic accident.

A car sped toward our stationary vehicle with terrifying speed, like a rhino charging in a frenzy.

Before My Breath is Scattered

Before we could react, the crash exploded behind us.

Our car shook violently, crumpling like paper at the back, and the impact left me dazed.

Only after everything stopped did I feel relief that we were still alive.

I kept calling out my daughter's name.

This crash took so much from me.

The force of the collision marked the beginning of a long journey involving two surgeries, repeated treatment injections, and harsh medications.

One part of my body became paralyzed in the process, and I began a new life as a person with a disability.

As time passed, the memories gradually started to fade.

Before My Breath is Scattered

This feeling of losing something little by little often left me disoriented.

However, even as I struggled physically and teetered between determination and despair, what kept me breathing was my daughter's existence.

Day by day, she grows healthier.

I cannot describe how much comfort that fact brings me.

Each time I see her smile or witness her growing, I rediscover the meaning of being alive.

And in June of 2024,

The cold impact of metal struck again.

Yet another car accident.

From the first rear-collision, my body and mind had already sustained deep wounds, and those wounds had long since become part of my daily life.

I had learned how to live with my disability, but the journey had been nothing short of agony.

Yet this second rear-accident toppled everything I had built, like a sandcastle swept away by the tide.

Once again, with the sound of metal colliding with metal, the fragile balance of my life was shattered.

Everything in front of me blurred as I found myself crashing down once more.

At the Hospital ER

The police and ambulance arrived, and I was transported to the hospital's

Before My Breath is Scattered

emergency room, where the stark white ceiling greeted me.

Though this scene had become familiar after the first accident, this time, an unbearable sense of despair overwhelmed me.

My body felt as though it had betrayed me, something I could no longer trust. My heart raced so violently that even the machines struggled to monitor its rhythm, and fear gripped me so tightly I began to vomit.

My body trembled uncontrollably from the sudden chill, and I couldn't stop the tears that flowed against my will.

The ER doctors and nurses quickly administered a powerful sedative along with strong painkillers to quell both the fear and the pain.

In about 20 minutes, as the medication spread through my body, my eyelids grew heavy, and I felt myself sinking into a lethargy.

For the first time, I couldn't consciously acknowledge my daughter's presence.

Even in that brief moment of calm, the paralysis and helplessness felt like shackles, weighing down my very being.

Being Alive

The fact that I am still breathing serves as a testament to the possibilities left within me.

Before My Breath is Scattered

Though I feel trapped in darkness, suffocated by helplessness, I pray that this is not my permanent stop, for I long to hold my daughter's hand again.

Anxiety consumes me, overpowering both my persona and body, holding me captive.

The shock of watching my life crumble again feels like an insurmountable wall.

Before completely losing my grip on reality that day, I tried to calm myself by writing, but in the end, I erased everything.

I think of my daughter, the one who keeps me breathing.

I must endure for her, though it is unbearably difficult.

Presently, I am living in extreme anxiety, enduring intense physical pain from the second car accident.

I take the painkillers, but will deny tranquilizers, fighting to regain my focus without them, but the process is anything but easy.

Still, I refuse to give up. This is why I remain resolute in resisting dependence on tranquilizers.

Amidst the Endless Pain

Doctor's appointments, treatments, injections, painkillers, tranquilizers, surgeries—all restarted after this second accident.

The trauma, now worsened, only adds to my unease.

Before My Breath is Scattered

This relentless cycle intensifies my anxiety, and I feel a desperate urge to find something, anything, to calm myself. The only solution that comes to me is reading—focusing my eyes in an effort to keep my mind from drifting away completely.

Although my struggle to overcome this without tranquilizers is incredibly challenging, I cannot stop thinking of my daughter.

For her, I will not give up.

Before My Breath is Scattered

Peace in the Noise of Starbucks
(Trying Not to Rely on Tranquilizers 2)

8:00 AM...

As soon as I open my eyes, I glance out the window.

The familiar, bustling cityscape of Manhattan greets me.

Skyscrapers stretch into the sky, and I can see people rushing along the streets even in the early hours of the morning.

In my daily life, I always feel the pulse of this city.

Today, I just hope to get through the day without relying on tranquilizers.

Anxiety and pain slowly approach, but at times, they seem to surge all at once, in waves of agony. I plead desperately to make it through this hurdle without medication.

11:00 AM

A sudden wave of anxiety overwhelms me. That heavy feeling sometimes comes without warning, binding me.
In that moment, with my bear coffee-stopper, I grab my book, along with my crutches, pack my bag, and slowly head toward the nearby Starbucks.
I hope to find some peace of mind amidst the warmth of coffee and the comforting sounds of people around me.

As soon as I entered Starbucks, the aroma of coffee embraced me.

Before My Breath is Scattered

The familiar scent brought a moment of relief.
At the counter, I ordered my usual hot Americano.

With only water and espresso combined, I believed that warm sip would briefly calm the anxiety rising within me.
As I waited for my name to be called, I realized that the noise of this place actually helped to calm me.

The chatter of people, the buzzing of the coffee machines, the steaming sound of milk foam, and the busy movements of the baristas seemed to firmly anchor me to reality.

Before My Breath is Scattered

Finally, my name was called.

Just as I stood up, the staff, seeing that I was disabled, told me they would bring it to me.

I took the hot paper cup in one hand and sat by the window.

Before My Breath is Scattered

Sunlight streamed in through the glass, and outside, people bustled toward their own lives.
I slowly took a sip of the Americano.
The warm liquid filled my mouth and traveled down my throat, spreading deeply inside my body.
In this moment, the warmth of the drink wrapped me up like a blanket, bringing peace.

I then took out a book and opened it.
I gazed at a familiar page, but for a moment, my thoughts became muddled.
I took a deep breath and slowly exhaled, trying to focus on the present moment.
I repeated the words to myself, reading them quietly in my head.

As I became aware of the people sitting around me, my body and mind slowly began to relax, in tune with the calm rhythm of my breathing.

Did 30 to 40 minutes pass? Perhaps a little more?
I observed the people passing by as I gazed out the window, sometimes focusing on the book, continuously trying to reclaim my peace.
Even the busyness outside seemed to give me a sense of stability just by watching it.
As I sat there, I felt like I was part of that flow, like a small droplet in a massive river, experiencing tranquility.

Before My Breath is Scattered

As lunchtime approached, a slight fatigue began to settle in.
But today, even that fatigue felt like a gift.
The fact that I could feel this calm without relying on tranquilizers was significant proof for me...

I put the book-filled bag over my shoulder, carefully placed the cup holder into the coffee cup to prevent spills, then held it in one hand while gripping my crutch with the other. Slowly, I walked out of Starbucks.
When I returned home, I turned on my Mac and sat in the chair.
I must have dozed off for a bit.

Before My Breath is Scattered

When I woke, I remained sitting in the chair.

Taking slow, deep breaths, I began to write about the moments my heart was feeling.

All the moments of daily life gathered together, supporting me and giving me the courage to face the things I fear.

Today, I lived through the day without tranquilizers, taking only the painkillers prescribed by the doctor for the pain from the second car accident.

Despite my efforts to forget, some memories from that day continue to haunt me:

About 20 minutes after taking several painkillers and some tranquilizers they said were "muscle relaxers," the effects of the medication spread through my body, leaving me lethargic and numb.

The presence of my daughter, which I couldn't erase even during the pain and hardship, seemed to fade away at that moment.

Everything became dull and confusing, and I was suddenly terrified of turning to a state where I couldn't control myself.

I still remember that moment.

I didn't want to let go of my consciousness while in the warm comfort of the medication.

I made the decision to endure reality as it is, without escaping it.

Before My Breath is Scattered

I want to face all this pain without relying on the medicine prescribed by the doctor.

Living each day won't be easy.

But I will continue to reject the tempting comfort of weakness and keep rejecting it.

I am determined to hold onto myself tightly, making sure my mind and spirit aren't consumed by the drugs.

No matter how difficult this path may be, I am determined to endure and live each day without relying on tranquilizers.

Today Marks 98 Days
(Trying Not to Rely on Tranquilizers 3)

The trauma from the June 2024 collision left deeper emotional scars and mental anguish than physical injuries.

On the day of the accident, I was administered three doses of painkillers and two doses of strong tranquilizers in the emergency room.

From that experience, I quickly decided I would no longer rely on tranquilizers.

Since then, each day has become a quiet battle. A fight within myself—a silent but relentless struggle to resist becoming dependent on those drugs.

Before My Breath is Scattered

Whenever anxiety unexpectedly creeps in, I try to soothe myself. I repeat to myself:
"It's going to be okay. Just endure this moment. You have to endure it. The moment you take those pills, it's all over. After that, you could become another addict, hunched over and dependent."
It's a path that's anything but easy.
Yet I hold on, day by day, slowly drawing resilience from the resolve within me.
And today, I trust it will sustain me once more.

And now, it has been 98 days.
My mind and spirit often scatter like petals in the wind.

Before My Breath is Scattered

I torment myself by worrying about a future that hasn't yet arrived or revisiting a past that's already slipped away.

"What if another accident happens? What if I have to endure this pain indefinitely?"—these thoughts haunt me incessantly.

But the real issue is this: None of these worries have materialized yet.

And most likely, they never will.

Still, accepting this truth has been anything but easy.

Sometimes, regrets about the past seize me.

"Why did I go there? What if I had just gone straight home that day?" These thoughts surface, but no matter how much I dwell on them, what has passed cannot be undone.

Whether it was the accident a few months ago or the one several years ago, the truth remains: What's done is beyond my control.

Because I cannot change the past, there is no need to hold onto it or let it torment me.

Regrets about what's gone and worries about what hasn't yet come only serve to render a present but powerless self. And so, I make efforts to let them go.

When my thoughts drift back to past accidents or begins to worry about a future that has yet to unfold, I ask myself:

"What is it that I can do right now?"

Asking this question seems to gradually pull me away from the grip of anxiety, giving me a chance to see the present moment more clearly.

Focusing on the now is the only choice, the one way I can help myself. It is something only I can do for me.

Focusing on the now feels like setting down a heavy burden.

As the weight lessens, I can finally breathe a little easier and see this very moment more clearly.

Clinging to the past or fearing the future only drains me.

Before My Breath is Scattered

It has become clear that the most practical way to protect myself is to focus solely on what I can do right now.

The past cannot be undone.
The future cannot be predicted.
But I can feel that this moment, the one I am standing in right now, truly belongs to me.
When I focus on the present, a sense of true freedom and calm begins to emerge.
It is in this state that I can finally live as my whole, unshaken self.
In that space, I find an opportunity—
A chance to step away from regret and anxiety, and to truly calm my mind.

Don't Buy Thoughts of Worry Like I Do in Life
(Trying Not to Rely on Tranquilizers 4)

Every moment spent on the road fills me with apprehension.

The memories of accidents rise like lingering afterimages, and the fear of "What if I get into another accident?" constantly overwhelms me.

Every time I get in the car, anxiety dominates, as though misfortune is lurking just ahead.

I wonder if an unexpected accident will strike again, and that worry refuses to leave me, even after I've left the road.

Before My Breath is Scattered

The worries I carry are not just simple anxieties.

They are heavy, like a burden I must bear, and they crush me as I imagine things that haven't happened yet.

The disabilities, paralysis, and trauma from two accidents, the ongoing treatment for six years, and the experience of facing death four times…

All those memories capture me, trapping me in them, while endless worry builds up inside me.

But as time passed, I realized something. All those worries were ultimately things I had conjured up myself.

My thoughts, endless worries that filled me—things I couldn't control—were exhausting me.

I had been buying into those worries with my heart and paying for them with my soul.

Unnecessary anxiety and fear were things I had created on my own, settling in my heart like never-ending bills, mentally disrupting my daily life.

And I had become so accustomed to that heavy burden.

I spent 129 days without tranquilizers. Though each day during that time was difficult, it was also a process of gradually realizing just how heavy those worries and thoughts had made me.

Before My Breath is Scattered

That heaviness was my choice, and shedding it wasn't as easy as I had imagined.

"Don't worry. Don't think about it," I told myself. I understood it in my head, but it was far too difficult to practice in my heart.

Moments of temptation often found me. When my thoughts became overwhelmed and complicated, I knew that just one pill of a tranquilizer would quiet everything, but I endured that temptation.

That one pill of calm was only temporary, and I was facing my confusion in order to find true peace.

Before My Breath is Scattered

129 days. I've endured well so far, and I will continue to do so.

This painful moment right now is just something I must bear.

Even if I don't know the way to where I'm heading and the end is not in sight, I will try to believe.

Someday, after passing through this long journey, there will be a day when I won't even think of tranquilizers, and I will be grateful to the version of myself who endured through my own strength.

Anxiety and pain may weigh me down, and at times, it may be hard to see ahead, but even in those moments, I can still recognize who I am.

When this pain passes, I will be stronger...

Rather than thinking of past accidents or future anxieties, I will focus on each small breath-by-breath in the present.

Sometimes, heavy emotions may come, but I practice simply observing and letting them go.

People often suggest relying on doctor-prescribed medication, but I think differently.

These medications are highly addictive and can lead to physical and psychological dependence.

Over time, more and more of the medication is needed to achieve the same effect, and when trying to stop, withdrawal symptoms can worsen anxiety and insomnia.

I was sincerely afraid of this, because I might lose sight of my daughter, the one who helps me breathe.

So, whenever there is a moment when I might need medication, what matters more is finding a way for my spirit not to rely on it.

The strength of my spirit—that is my most important weapon.

If I believe in that strength and continue to refine it, I can walk this path to the end.

One day, when I reach the end of this tunnel, I will realize something.

Before My Breath is Scattered

Even in that darkness, I never collapsed...
The fact that I believed in myself and walked this far will make me stronger.
And when that day comes, I will no longer think of the word "tranquilizer."

Whenever my thoughts and spirit felt unsettled, I made an effort to bring myself back to the present moment.
When anxiety and worry overwhelmed me, I would repeat this question to myself like a mantra:
"What can I do right now?"
That question brought me back to the present.
It was like a small compass that guided me, even amid the tangled emotions.

Before My Breath is Scattered

I found my way to the answer and left behind 100 pieces of writing as traces of my journey.

Life Unfolds Through Encounters

In Buddhism, it is said that none of our encounters are mere coincidences; they are the result of karma and the connections we have accumulated across past and present lives. It is believed that we have crossed paths over three thousand times in previous lives, which is why even the smallest encounters in this life carry profound significance. From the moment we are born until the day we die, we experience countless interactions. Among them, some leave a lasting impact and stay with us for a lifetime, while others may seem as fleeting as the wind brushing past. Yet, as time passes, we come to understand that even those brief encounters have left their traces on our lives. There are various forms of encounters:

1. Destiny (인연/因緣):
Relationships between people are not random occurrences but inevitable meetings shaped by past actions and their consequences. The people we meet are a reflection of the actions and choices we have made in the past, leading to the formation of these encounters.

2. Negative Fate (악연/惡緣):
Although these relationships bring conflict and pain, Buddhism views them as opportunities for growth and learning.

Negative karma serves as a necessary experience for personal development and maturity.

3. Inevitability (필연/必然):
These are destined encounters that are bound to happen. We cannot escape them, and through these meetings, we gain valuable life lessons.

4. Coincidence (우연/偶然):
Unpredictable and unexpected encounters that may initially seem insignificant but reveal their importance over time. Such meetings can bring unforeseen changes, ultimately proving to hold great meaning in our lives.

5.   Heavenly Match (천생연분/天生緣分):
A special connection destined by the heavens, often interpreted as fated love. These encounters are inevitable and profound, representing a unique bond that transcends choice.

In my life, there was such an encounter. Without warning, a car accident abruptly entered my world. That accident completely upended everything. The person responsible was a stranger—a person I had never met before. Because of their mistake, I endured days of pain, suffering, and despair. Eventually, I became disabled.

Before My Breath is Scattered

At first, I resented the person who caused the accident. My once-healthy body and normal life were shattered in an instant, and the pain, both physical and emotional, left me feeling powerless. I thought, "If it weren't for them, I wouldn't be suffering like this." Was that encounter with the perpetrator the result of negative karma? Or was it simply bad luck, being in the wrong place at the wrong time? I couldn't understand why such misfortune had to happen to me.

But as time passed, I began to think differently. The pain forced me to look inward, and gradually, I found strength within myself, refusing to give up. More than anything, seeing my daughter grow gave me the resolve to keep pushing forward. The suffering helped me mature and revealed parts of myself I hadn't known before.

Through this accident, I came to understand that the person who caused it was part of a natural course I had to face—an element of life's inherent order. As a result, I began to accept the accident not just as negative fate, but as an essential part of my journey. Though the encounter caused me pain, it was through that pain that I found personal growth.

In life, accidents and suffering often come unexpectedly. We might see them only as painful burdens, believing there is no way to escape the anguish they bring. But as time passes, these experiences offer us opportunities to learn and grow. What matters is how we choose to face that pain and whether we can use it to build resilience.

Every experience in life leads to encounters that shape us, and ultimately, those encounters become what make us who we are.

Each event and meeting holds intrinsic value, and it's only by seeking meaning in them that we come to understand how these encounters form the pieces of our life's puzzle. It is through all of life's experiences that we create meaningful connections, and in the end, these connections shape who we are.

Before My Breath is Scattered

SCRIBBLED EMOTIONS
DAY BY DAY:

Day 1 - Life

Living life, there are things that come unexpectedly.

For reasons I didn't foresee, they approach my life.

Thus, I may find myself cornered or pushed to my limits.

I may experience pain.

However, if there is one reason to live, if I seek that one purpose, it can be expressed as the beginning of the strength to live.

Day 2 - Appreciating

I simply want to sit in a chair and write, but I can't. The pain is unbearable. Even the potent painkillers prescribed by the doctor are of no use. I feel disconnected from a normal life, unable to grasp its essential values. Now, in the midst of this agony, I realize my own ignorance—the witlessness of not appreciating the simple, normal life I once took for granted.

Day 3 - Wounds

The wounds inflicted by others spring from our shared humanity. They are the price of understanding, the cost of uncovering the depths of what it means to be human. In the end, these scars mark the path that leads us to each other.

Day 4 - Moment

Though worry persists, distress lingers;
Though reflection deepens, thoughts multiply.
In this moment, we need nothing but to act.

Not to fall into anguish, not to stop,
Not to stay lost in thought—
Just take one small step.

Perfection isn't necessary.
What matters is moving forward, without pause.

Day 5 - Wrap

Wrapped in love, judgment clouds, they marry.

Lacking understanding, consumed by conflicts, they divorce.

Time passes, memories fade, and the reasons dissolve

as they remarry.

Aging and buried in slowness they accept and go on living.

Day 6 - Existence

I am myself as I differ from others;

that is the essence of my existence.

In sameness, there is no specialness.

In difference, my light shines brighter.

Rather than follow a trail,

I walk my own path,

Not by others' standards,

but by my own.

Only then do I exist—completely as "Me."

Day 7 - Blame

Before love, we imagine things we cannot yet know.
When love begins, imagination becomes reality—indescribably beautiful, beyond words.

As time passes, and we grow accustomed, we begin to see the other differently.
What once thrilled us and felt special now becomes buried in familiarity,
and sometimes even feels dull.

In those moments, we blame each other, saying,
"You're not like before."

But the truth is, it's not the other person who has changed—

it's our perspective, our mindset.

If respect can remain, the relationship will endure.

If not, it will inevitably drift apart.

Day 8 - Relationship

In human relationships,

are days like seasonal clothes—times we need to clean and sort.

Days where like trees—times we need to leave alone.

Days like the six feet of social distancing—times we need to appropriately distance.

In human relationships, I hope for no heartaches.

Day 9 - Character

I shape my own character.

The beauty of a flower blooms within my heart.

My heart becomes a light that illuminates the world,

and through it, I see the world.

Like petals unfolding, the goodness within me forms my character.

Through that figure, I recognize beauty.

Depending on the heart I hold,

my world transforms,

and in that world, I shape myself.

Day 10 - Like That

Life is without preview.

Life is without practice.

To be clumsy,

to be wrong,

to be lacking are alright.

In the past,

without being bound,

without regret,

faithful to the present,

in that look,

like that,

you can live.

Day 11 - Difference Between Pain and Suffering

When a scraped knee

sheds a single drop of blood,

pain whispers:

"It stings now, but it will heal soon."

But suffering

comes quietly,

nesting deep in the chest,

drawing out its sharp blades without

reason.

Pain passes through the body,

without leaving scars,

but suffering traverses the heart,

casting deep shadows.

Before My Breath is Scattered

Pain flows with time,

while suffering clings to time,

weeping silently.

In the end, we understand:

Pain is the storm that will pass,

while suffering is an inner stone,

we must eventually remove.

Day 12 - Rest

On some days not meeting anyone

weary from human relationships,

I can gift myself great rest.

On some days putting everything down

immersed in meditation

troubled by human relationships

I can purify myself with great peace.

Day 13 - Play

When your child wants to play with you, you feel annoyed. You hand your phone to your child.

When you are old and want to spend time with your child, your child will hand the phone to you.

Day 14 - Now

We must deeply realize the truth that this very moment is all we truly have.
We often live by planning for the future and reflecting on the past.
Yet, within that flow of time, we often forget the essence of the present.
We let slip the moment called "now."

So, what is it that grants us true value?
It is none other than a single point beyond the construct of time—the present.
The past has already gone, and the future has yet to arrive.
All we are given is this moment—now, the entirety of what we possess.

Before My Breath is Scattered

We often unconsciously try to hold on to time.

As if doing so would help us live a better life.

But clinging to time is nothing but an illusion.

It does not linger in our hands for even a moment,

constantly brushing past us.

What we must treasure is not the mere passage of time.

Rather, it is this very moment,

now, that exists within the flow of time,

moment by fleeting moment,

which holds the true value.

Where should the focus of life lie?

Before My Breath is Scattered

We always try to find the answer outside of ourselves.

But the true focus of life is always within us.

When we fully immerse ourselves in the moment called now,

we are no longer pursued by time.

In this moment,

we are finally free.

Day 15 - Much

Someone knows as much as they see,

Speaks as much as they know.

Believing that only what is visible is everything,

Trying to understand the world within it.

But true wisdom

Comes from feeling the unseen,

From understanding depth without words.

What is seen and known is not everything,

Don't fear the unknown,

A heart that seeks to understand more

Leads to true knowledge.

Day 16 - Again

In human relationships,

if it's someone you'll never see again,

there's no need to worry.

But if there's a chance you'll meet them again,

offering honest and fair feedback

can help maintain a good relationship.

Day 17 - One Thing

Living with a disability is full of hardship,

but giving up on life will feel too regretful.

That regret is outweighed by one thing—my daughter, who is like oxygen to me.

Day 18 - Boundary Between Tears & Sorrow

Tears flow,

but sorrow lingers.

Tears, like a fleeting stream,

rush past and leave traces behind,

while sorrow, like a deep lake,

settles quietly in one corner of the heart.

Tears are a confession.

They hold the wounds of the day

and the unspoken pains,

falling in clear drops.

Sorrow is silence.

In the dried trails of tears,

Before My Breath is Scattered

it remains without a word,

growing deeper with time.

Tears can be shed and let go,

but sorrow must be held.

Tears eventually dry,

but sorrow seeps in,

filling the core of our being.

And so, we wash away sorrow in our tears

and seek tears within our sorrow.

Though they are different,

together they make us human.

Day 19 - Head

The head is not a mere display shelf.

It's not just for placing a hat

Or decorating with hair.

Words spoken without thought,

That hold human relationships together,

Can in an instant, shatter the

fundamental trust.

Day 20 - Gone

Joys together have disappeared but suffering by that person have also gone. Someone to hand me a hot cup of tea when sick, disappeared, including more heartaches by that someone.

Day 21 - Strong

It is not the strong who survive in life,
but the survivor who is strong.

Some try to conquer the world with strength,
True strength is the ability to endure it
With the courage to stand up again.

Those who collide and fall,
Who rebuild themselves after crumbling,
Are ultimately the strongest.

Only those who survive
Can lead the change in the world.

Day 22 - Next

Without waiting,

the next season arrives.

Even while holding on,

the next season changes.

Even human relationships—

fated connections,

like approaching seasons;

parting destinies,

like changing seasons.

Day 23 - Last

When I take my last breath,

When I die,

Please don't place me in a coffin.

I fear being trapped in a small, stifling space.

When I die,

Please don't bury me in the ground.

The cold earth will chill my heart,

And the darkness fill me with fear,

Like I'm suffocating.

Cremate me,

Turn me into ashes.

And on a day when the wind blows,

Scatter me over the wide ocean.

Before My Breath is Scattered

Let me dissolve into the waves,

Carried by the breeze,

Flowing endlessly,

Breathing again, forever free.

Day 24 - I Write

I do not write for the sake of record keeping.

Four times at death's door,

Two car collisions.

Lying on the operating table,

Six years of physical therapy.

Paralysis and disability,

Unending trauma.

Pain I struggle to endure

Without sedatives or tranquilizers.

And yet, amidst it all,

I strive not to lose myself.

Amid the pitying gazes,

I want to find my true self.

The reason I continue living—

She is here.

Before My Breath is Scattered

Every time I hold her tiny hand,

The warmth of the world flows into me.

Through her,

My life shines once more.

My daughter is my breath,

My center.

And so, I write.

To keep pain and love

From scattering into the wind.

Writing is the quiet breath

That carries my life forward.

Day 25 - First Snow

The proverb "If you meet someone when the first snow falls, you will have eternal love" is a Korean saying that means that meeting someone on that special day creates a bond that lasts long.

Then should we ask a loved one, "Shall we meet on the day the first snow falls?"

Day 26 - Alone!

Alone, do not just endure and endure!

Alone, even swear!

Alone, try shouting out loud!

Alone, cry sorrowfully!

Spit out all that's piled up,

and live again by filling yourself up

with good things!

Day 27 - Your Choice

If that is where your heart stands,

isn't that enough?

The measures of right and wrong are

meaningless,

and your choice alone should be enough.

Whatever the reason,

the hesitation,

the wavering—

it all becomes part of your story,

embracing and enfolding your decision.

A step forward in the dark,

a bold stride toward the light—

every single one is a choice that makes

you, you.

Before My Breath is Scattered

So, trust yourself.

The path you've chosen will become your own,

shining brightly under the vast sky.

Day 28 - Holding

At times unmoved,

At times apathetically,

At times dismissing,

Holding it within,

Your heart will only suffer.

Caught at my fingertips,

the weight of separation,

Can't let go—the tighter you hold,

The scars get deeper.

Shaking, indifference, avoidance—

Ultimately just gestures deceiving oneself.

True healing

Begins with the courage to let go.

Before My Breath is Scattered

Embracing pain,

The moment you gently open your hand,

Only then the heart

Becomes free.

Before My Breath is Scattered

Day 29 - Reaction

After the car accident,

as I was carried into the ER in an ambulance,

they gave me a tranquilizer to calm me.

Staring at the white ceiling,

I suddenly began wrestling with a question.

Why do people live?

My mind grew more and more tangled.

Is it for happiness? For success? For love?

I considered reasons that seemed plausible,

but a sense of emptiness lingered in my heart.

Before My Breath is Scattered

Then it dawned on me.

The reason doesn't have to be grand.

Isn't it simply because I was born and am still alive?

Life is that simple.

Just by the fact that we are breathing,

We already have a reason to live.

We don't have to look for complicated reasons.

Because just being alive at this moment is enough reason to continue living.

Before My Breath is Scattered

Day 30 - Even Tonight

I wish the pain would disappear.

I wish the agony would subside.

If only the torment and worries were gone,

then this moment of just breathing would feel a bit lighter.

I don't even look forward to tomorrow.

If I can sleep comfortably tonight,

that's enough.

I wish the sadness would disappear.

I wish the hollow emptiness of loneliness would fade.

If only the tension would ease,

if fear would quiet down,

how much better it would be.

Before My Breath is Scattered

If I could rest without worrying about tomorrow,

if my heart could feel lighter tonight,

if I could close my eyes peacefully,

that would be enough.

I wish the dizziness would stop.

I wish my wounds would heal.

If I could be okay even on my own,

if the anxiety would leave,

if I could believe that tomorrow might be slightly better than today,

if I could simply rest tonight,

that would be enough.

I wish the pain would cease.

I wish my restless heart would calm.

If only the worries would leave,

Before My Breath is Scattered

for hope to rise once more.

If tomorrow could come without fear,

if I could fall asleep peacefully

tonight,

that would be enough.

Then, I could endure whatever moments

tomorrow may bring.

Day 31 - Expectation

When expectations stretch up like a giraffe,

Disappointments tower the same.

When aspirations are tiny like an ant,

Disappointments shrink to its size

But neither too low

nor too high,

Balancing expectations and aspirations,

That is likely

The way to keep a peaceful heart.

Day 32 - Same

There are many similar people in the world

yet none are identical

Some even think like me

but are never the same person

When you force different things into sameness

Like same-sided magnets

repulsion occurs

Day 33 - Pain

I should have smiled more back then,

I should have loved more,

I should have forgiven more,

Or just,

I should have just stayed a little longer.

Anything in life

Is ultimately forgotten,

As living becomes too busy.

So much time flows,

All traces disappear,

While regretful pain lingers.

Day 34 - Irony

Where does it end? When will the pain subside?
Through the searing agony—like bones being shaved, flesh torn away—
I asked again and again.
But no one answered,
and time steeped in pain flowed forward, without any response.

My body burned with suffering.
Each breath, heavy and scorching, mingled with sweat and tears.
Groans escaped my lips as I wandered, searching for an end.

Before My Breath is Scattered

The end never came. Instead, parts of me began to lose feeling.

Numbness. Paralysis.

And in the stillness of that deadened sensation,

a strange fear arose:

a life without pain felt lifeless.

Pain was torment, but it made me feel alive.

Without it, the calm dulled even the essence of living.

An irony:

I, who had fought so hard to feel life through pain,

now faced a deeper void in its absence.

Then I realized:

Before My Breath is Scattered

This expedition is not one of endings.

It is a road of acceptance.

Pain or calm, feeling or numbness,

I must carry them all and keep moving.

On this road, I walk again today.

Not seeking the end,

but finding meaning in every step

forward,

holding even my pain close as I live on.

Day 35 - Human

In human relationships without anything obvious, everything can be an exception.

When the boundaries between each other blur,
And expectations become vague,
Any words or actions
Can be interpreted in different ways.

Without standards,
It is difficult to understand each other's feelings,
And impossible to know where things went wrong.

There must be clear lines with respect,

Before My Breath is Scattered

For true relationships to be formed,

And within that, we can understand each other,

And build trust.

Day 36 - Thought's End?

Thoughts are infinite.

But actions transform that infinity into reality.

No matter how many worries or plans we have,

if we do not act, nothing will change.

Actions may be imperfect,

but even that imperfection brings about transformation.

In the end, thought can never surpass action.

What propels us forward is a single small step.

Day 37 - The Boundary Between Emotion and Attitude

Emotion is momentary, but attitude is enduring.
We may raise our voices in anger,
but if we adopt that anger as an attitude,
we will always appear sharp and on edge before others.
It is natural to be steeped in sadness,
but if we accept that sadness as a way of life,
we risk viewing everything with cynicism.

Emotions are best left in their moment.
To feel joy, anger, sadness as they are,
and then to let them pass.

But the moment emotion solidifies into attitude,

we begin to distort life through the prism of that emotion.

When someone's tone feels harsh and anger flares,

I must ensure that anger does not become my attitude,

causing me to treat them coldly.

Even when overwhelming sadness tries to consume me,

I must take care not to let that sadness blanket my entire life.

Emotions are the fierce light that makes us feel alive,

Before My Breath is Scattered

but attitude is the window through which we view the world.

To keep the light from obscuring the window,

to ensure that emotion does not cross into the realm of attitude.

Day 38 - Let Go

Let go of perfectionism to grasp peace of mind.

When pursuing perfection,
The endless road only increases anxiety.
Trying to make everything perfect,
You lose yourself,
And peace is lost from it.

However, in letting go,
Freedom and peace come.
When accepting imperfection
And truly loving oneself within it,
True peace of heart can be found

Day 39 - Laugh

When you're happy, you laugh.

When you're sad, you laugh even harder,

to hide the sorrow.

In that smile,

Silence that might shatter,

Tears ready to fall,

Breathe together.

Unnoticed,

Buried in the corner of my heart,

Covered with laughter,

That endless sadness

Echoes from deep inside.

So eventually,

Before My Breath is Scattered

Let go that sorrow.

A day to quietly comfort

Will find me.

Day 40 - Habit

Whatever they may be, I like quiet things.

Whatever they may be, I like simple things.

Whatever they may be, I like observing things.

Whatever they may be, I like flat things.

Maybe it's because I've been living a life of lying down since the car accident. I guess I've become awkward when it comes to connecting to three-dimensional things...

Day 41 - Position

When I walk along the streets, and pass by or see someone struggling physically, I would feel a sense of pity, sometimes even condescension. Now, finding myself in the same position as those who suffer, I discover that others can see me with that feeling of pity as well.

Day 42 - Interpretation

If a loved one nags you,

some may see it as a sign of care,

while others may take it as interference or stress.

If a loved one is silent,

some may see it as consideration,

while others may feel ignored.

If a loved one frequently contacts you,

some may see it as affection,

while others may see it as obsession.

If a loved one occasionally needs distance,

some may understand it as needing personal time,
while others may interpret it as a sign of drifting apart.

If a loved one expresses emotions honestly,
some may see it as sincerity,
while others may feel hurt.

If a loved one avoids addressing issues,
some may see it as an effort not to complicate things,
while others may see it as avoiding responsibility.

If a loved one asks for help,

some may see it as trust to share

burdens,

while others may see it as dependency.

Day 43 - See

To those who see only what is visible,

the unseen heart remains a mystery.

Hidden behind appearances,

Are deep stories,

Beyond their gaze,

Sincerity,

With frivolous words,

Never reaches them.

To understand that mystery,

Not with the eyes,

Look with the heart.

True communication.

What is unseen,

Begins from feeling.

Day 44 - Difference?

I don't have a boyfriend, but I have a friend who just broke up with hers.
I'm not married, but I have a friend whose marriage fell apart.
I don't have a job, but I have a friend who lost hers.
I don't have much money, but I have a friend who lost everything in the stock market.
I'm not lonely on my own, but I have a friend who, despite being with someone, feels alone.

And I wonder—what's the difference?

Day 45 - Expression

Smile to hide your sorrow at times,

Remain expressionless

To mask the guilt of your joy.

A smile, sometimes,

Drawn over dried tears,

Expressionless,

Becomes a wall to suppress the excited heart.

Thus, we

Wrap our emotions in visible faces,

With unseen hearts,

We fight alone.

But someday,

Before My Breath is Scattered

The courage to face our true emotions

May gift us with peace.

Day 46 - Traces

The traces people leave on my day:
When I meet good people, my day brightens.
When I meet bad people, it turns cloudy.
That's why meeting people holds great significance in life.
We become a part of each other's lives,
just as they become a part of ours.
The people who fill my days,
and the traces I leave behind in theirs,
are all precious.

Before My Breath is Scattered

Day 47 - Find Me

I underwent surgery,

took medication,

received injections—

I thought I'd get better.

I thought the pain would lessen.

I thought the suffering would ease.

I thought the agony would fade.

But it didn't.

The pain returned, different, unfamiliar.

It evaded all those treatments,

and came to find me,

settling into my body.

Day 48 - On Three Legs

One step, then another,

the third leg always lifts me

back up again.

Where has the world of running on two

legs gone?

Now, I must tread this path

on three legs alone.

The first leg touches the ground,

the second pushes me forward,

and the third catches me,

urging me to continue, again and again.

Before My Breath is Scattered

Even when cold winds brush against my face, the steady rhythm of my three-legged stride
finds its strength in every footprint.

A path that must be walked on three legs—
will a flower bloom at its end,
waiting for me?

But no matter what,
I will walk on three legs.
It is how I live,
and it is why I keep rising.

Before My Breath is Scattered

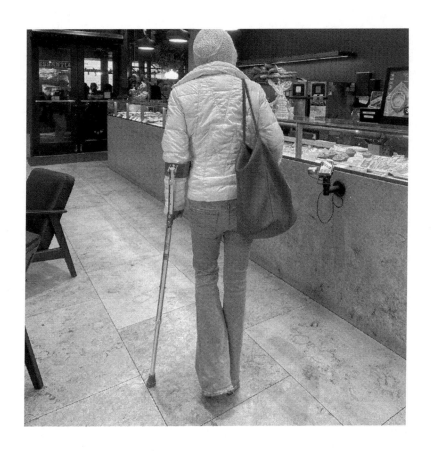

Before My Breath is Scattered

"Thanks to you,

my imperfections find meaning

in being read."

ABOUT THE AUTHOR

Kimisoo Kim is a Korean American who majored in Fashion Design at Parsons School of Design, The New School.

Upon graduation, her career began with an internship at Anna Sui. Her path as a professional designer was solidified with experience at prestigious brands such as Polo Ralph Lauren, Ann Taylor Loft, Target Private Label, and more. Her story has been featured in The New York Daily News and Time Out New York Magazine.

However, the glamorous life she once led in the bustling city vanished in an instant. After marrying and giving birth to her daughter, her life veered in an entirely unexpected direction. She moved to a place where she was unknown, beginning what she describes as the life of "Mommy Papillon."

Six years later, after returning to her life in New York City, this chapter of her life was also dramatically disrupted by an unforeseen trial when a car accident left her disabled. Yet again, in 2024, a second accident struck.

Until that moment, she had been fighting to heal from the physical and emotional scars of her past. However, this second shock marked a significant turning point in her journey.

After the first accident, as she endured days of pain and suffering, writing became her compass—a guiding force that preserved her sense of self.

Kim shares her second book of writings here, hoping to inspire others through reflection and resilience.